The forces of nature . . .

Liane struck his hand away, suddenly furious. "I don't have to take this, Jake! If you think so little of me, why do you keep on kissing me as though I'm the last woman on earth, and why the hell did you bother tracking me down all the way from the Wentwork Valley to here?"

"If I knew the answer to that question, I probably wouldn't be here!"

"Then let me make something clear. If you think you're going to have a cozy little affair with me in return for watching over Patrick, you're quite wrong. That's not in the cards. I don't have affairs—the cost's too high! So if that's why you're here, now's your chance to leave."

SANDRA FIELD, once a biology technician, now writes full-time under the pen names of Jocelyn Haley and Jan MacLean. She lives with her son in Canada's Maritimes, which she often uses as a setting for her books. She loves the independent lifestyle she has as a writer. She's her own boss, sets her own hours and increasingly there are travel opportunities.

Books by Sandra Field

HARLEQUIN PRESENTS
1280—GOODBYE FOREVER
1336—LOVE AT FIRST SIGHT
1416—THE LAND OF MAYBE
1448—HAPPY ENDING
1506—SAFETY IN NUMBERS

HARLEQUIN ROMANCE
2457—THE STORMS OF SPRING
2480—SIGHT OF A STRANGER
2577—THE TIDES OF SUMMER

writing as Jan MacLean
2295—EARLY SUMMER
2348—WHITE FIRE
2537—ALL OUR TOMORROWS

writing as Jocelyn Haley
DREAM OF DARKNESS

Don't miss any of our special offers. Write to us at the following address for information on our newest releases.

Harlequin Reader Service
P.O. Box 1397, Buffalo, NY 14240
Canadian address: P.O. Box 603,
Fort Erie, Ont. L2A 5X3

SANDRA FIELD

Taken by Storm

Harlequin Books

TORONTO • NEW YORK • LONDON
AMSTERDAM • PARIS • SYDNEY • HAMBURG
STOCKHOLM • ATHENS • TOKYO • MILAN
MADRID • WARSAW • BUDAPEST • AUCKLAND

For Dodie
With Love

Harlequin Presents first edition May 1993
ISBN 0-373-11557-1

Original hardcover edition published in 1992
by Mills & Boon Limited

TAKEN BY STORM

CHAPTER ONE

MONEY can do anything, Liane. Money can do anything at all.

Liane Daley leaned forward in the car seat, peering through the windshield where the wipers swished back and forth, back and forth, in a rhythm that should have been soothing and was not. For it was not rain that the wiper blades were clearing from her vision. It was snow. Small, thick, purposeful flakes of snow.

The snow had started falling that afternoon while she and her father had been talking in the formal living room of his big house by the sea. Liane turned the heater fan up another notch, her mouth twisting, for talk was a totally inadequate word to describe what had passed between her and Murray Hutchins behind doors carefully closed so that none of the servants would hear. Arguing would be a more accurate term. Although even arguing could not carry the full weight of that disastrous conversation that had ended with her father choleric and herself white-faced and terrified.

The word she used to describe that conversation did not really matter. By the time she had left Halifax two and a half hours ago it had been snowing heavily, and in ordinary circumstances she would never have set off on a journey that on the best of days could take five or six hours. But circumstances were not ordinary; no power on earth could have made her stay in that house.

So here she was a hundred miles from Halifax in the middle of the Wentworth Valley. She had skied here in her younger days on the slopes a few miles up the road.

5

It was a beautiful valley, with its rounded hills and its
beech and maple groves. It was also an area notorious
for heavy snowfalls and high winds, and right now Liane
would have given everything she owned to be on the
straight stretch of highway beyond the valley, heading
for the border between Nova Scotia and New Brunswick.
Heading for the ferry that would take her back to Prince
Edward Island and home. Home, where Patrick was.

Her hands tightened unconsciously on the wheel. She
could not afford to think about Patrick. Not now, when
keeping the car on the road required every ounce of her
concentration and skill.

The snow, which was dense and settling fast, had been
rutted and grooved by the traffic, and her car was a small
and venerable Volkswagen; if she got into the deep stuff,
she would be in trouble. A big gray Chevrolet was ahead
of her, and a nondescript dark blue car behind. She had
been between these two vehicles for at least an hour, and
had come to think of them as friends. Ahead of the
Chevrolet was a four-wheel-drive wagon in a cheerful
cherry red. If she were driving that, she thought envi-
ously, she wouldn't have a worry in the world.

The road had not been ploughed for at least an hour.
The ruts were getting deeper by the minute, and, worse,
the tracks worn by the tires were greasy with ice. A salt
truck, Liane thought longingly. A big green salt truck.
Or a nice yellow snowplow with its orange lights flashing.
Either one would do. She wasn't fussy.

The back end of the Chevrolet swung wildly from side
to side. Liane eased her foot off the accelerator. As the
Chevrolet straightened, she saw a small beige car halfway
in the ditch, its driver shoveling the mounds of snow
from under the back wheels. The beige car was the size
of hers; she bit her lip and increased her speed
fractionally.

Even though she had directed all the heat on to the windshield, the wipers were getting caked with ice, making smears in the glass. Tension banding her forehead, Liane hunched a little further over the wheel. Her feet were cold. But her feet would have to wait.

The digital clock on the dash flicked from six fifty-nine to seven o'clock. She was at least eighty miles from the ferry, and it was already getting dark. But at least it wasn't windy. The ferries would be running, and the flow of traffic from the ferry would carry her safely as far as the city of Charlottetown. She lived not far from there; she could surely manage the last few miles on her own.

The highway curved gently to the right, a high cliff looming on the far side. Then through the blurred white of the snow Liane saw the flash of yellow lights, and her heart lifted. The plow. Something being done to improve the atrocious condition of the road. Wonderful!

As quickly as they had risen, her spirits plummeted. The yellow lights were on two tow trucks clustered around a transport truck that had jackknifed into the ditch on the far side of the road, its cab leaning drunkenly against the granite face of the cliff. If a truck that size ever skidded toward her, she wouldn't stand a chance.

Nothing was going to happen, she told herself stoutly. As long as she followed the cherry red wagon and the gray Chevrolet, she would be all right.

Her tires whined on a patch of ice. The brake lights gleamed on the red wagon, and the Chevrolet followed suit. Liane shifted to second gear, then down to first, as the cars ahead of her slowed to a virtual crawl. Ten kilometres an hour, she thought despairingly. She'd never get home at this rate. Oh, Patrick...

Money can do anything, Liane. Money can do anything at all.

The worst thing about her present situation was that she herself had instigated this second visit with her father. Of her own free will. From the best of motives. Two weeks ago, when she had read of her brother Howard's death in the newspapers, she had gone to the funeral, taking Patrick with her. Howard and she had never been close—eleven years older and a replica of her father, Howard had always kept his sister at arm's length—so she had gone to the funeral more for her father's sake than for her brother's. This visit today, which she had undertaken alone, had been motivated by compassion for the small, shrunken man her father had become, for the bewilderment she had glimpsed beneath his pathetic composure at the funeral service, for the shakiness of old limbs under the immaculately tailored black suit. She had expected to give comfort today, and had hoped to give love; the reality, however, had not turned out that way at all.

Abruptly she came back to the present. There were more lights ahead of her, flashing through the shifting curtain of snow—red and blue lights this time. Police cars had red and blue lights.

An accident?

Her stomach tightened. That would explain why the traffic had slowed so suddenly a few minutes ago. Praying no one had been hurt, she inched forward.

The brake lights ahead of her snapped on again. The red wagon stopped. The Chevrolet pulled up behind it. Liane, gritting her teeth in mingled frustration and fear, also came to a halt.

Without the churning of packed snow between her wheels, the interior of the car seemed very quiet. The motor hummed away and the wipers swished across the glass. Then the driver of the Chevrolet got out of his car and walked toward the flashing lights of the police car. Liane sat still, paralyzed by indecision. If there was an accident, there would be a delay, a prolonged delay; if not, then why were they stopped?

Pulling on her gloves, she left the engine running and got out of the car. The snowflakes brushed her face, catching on her lashes and melting on her forehead as she trudged through the snow toward the red wagon. She was wearing very impractical knee-high leather boots, bought three winters ago on sale and cherished ever since, and a hip-length wool jacket in rose pink, also bought on sale; her entire outfit had been chosen to give her courage for the visit with her father rather than to protect her from the elements. Avoiding the deepest snow, feeling the cold air bite through her thin leather gloves, she passed the Chevrolet and saw a police officer in a bright orange coat standing in front of the red wagon. The driver of the wagon had rolled his window down to hear what the policeman was saying. The man from the Chevrolet was listening as well, his hands thrust in his pockets. To her infinite relief there did not appear to be any signs of an accident.

And then she heard what the police officer was saying. "Road closed, sir. We've arranged temporary accommodation at a school just up the road. If you'd return to your vehicle, my colleague up ahead will direct you. Thank you, sir."

"Damned nuisance," the Chevrolet driver blustered. "I've got an important meeting in Moncton."

"The highway's closed between the border and Moncton, too," the policeman said soothingly.

The man was not mollified. "A school? What kind of accommodation's that?"

"Best we can do in the circumstances, sir. Some of the local women are organizing a supper for you; you'll find it much more comfortable to stay there overnight than in your——"

Liane said blankly, "*Overnight?*"

"That's right, ma'am. The latest forecast is for the snow to continue until well past midnight, and we don't have enough plows to keep the road operable."

"But I can't stay overnight!"

"I'm afraid there's no other choice."

Patrick . . .

"I can't! It's impossible." Liane heard the edge of hysteria in her voice, and fought it down, the snow on her face and the chill in the air both forgotten in this greater peril. "I have to get back to Prince Edward Island tonight——"

"Ferries aren't operating, ma'am. If you'd please return to your vehicle so we can keep the traffic moving here . . ."

Liane could see his face in the alternating flashes of red and blue light: a young man with blond hair doing his job in very difficult circumstances. "Is there a telephone I can use?" she asked desperately. "I have to get a message through; it's extremely important!"

"At the school, ma'am. Providing the lines are still in operation."

From the red wagon behind Liane a clipped voice said, "Young lady, would you kindly return to your car so the rest of us can get inside in the warm?"

Liane turned in her tracks, the intensity of her anger in direct proportion to the intensity of her fear. "Would you kindly mind your own business?" she snapped.

"When you're holding up a whole line of traffic in a snowstorm, it is my business."

In the blue light his hair was black, in the red light auburn. In either light he was the most attractive man she had ever seen, and she disliked him on sight. Her cheeks pink from more than the cold, she opened her mouth to retaliate, and heard the man from the Chevrolet bluster, "Now that's no way to speak to a lady——"

The policeman said loudly, "Please return to your vehicles immediately. Sir——" this to the driver of the wagon "—would you follow the other car, please?"

The driver of the wagon, not bothering to give Liane a second glance, rolled up his window and began edging toward the second police car, which was parked a little further along the road. Had Liane been wearing her old hiking boots, she might well have stamped her foot; as it was, she gave the red wagon a dirty look and marched back to her car, slamming the door hard after she had got in. Insufferable man! He'd had no right to speak to her like that, no right at all.

In a clash of gears she surged up the slope, her mouth set mutinously. Of course she had complained when she was suddenly told she was not allowed to proceed to her destination; it had been a perfectly natural reaction...
And here her temper died, smothered by a flood of fear so strong that she forgot everything else: the interminable snowfall, the polite policeman, and the rude owner of the wagon. She would not get home tonight. She would, instead, be spending the night with a group of strangers in a country schoolhouse in the middle of a blizzard being fed soup and sandwiches by the local ladies. If her need to be at home were not so compelling, the situation would almost be funny.

The police car, lights still swirling in the gathering dusk, turned down a side road which had been plowed fairly recently, and which was flanked by spruce trees weighed down with snow, and by gaunt maples whose limbs touched fingers overhead. The road soon opened into a yard, in the middle of which was a one-story white-shingled school. Its windows were decorated, rather optimistically, with paper cutouts of scarlet tulips and yellow daffodils.

Liane parked beside the gray Chevrolet and shut off the ignition. A telephone, she thought numbly. I have to get to a telephone. She reached in the back seat for the small kit bag that she had used in the motel last night, looped her handbag over her shoulder, and got out of the Volkswagen just as the dark blue car parked beside her. Its driver was one of those undistinguished men one could pass in a crowd and never notice.

The second police officer, who looked even younger than the first one, waited until a dozen or so cars had trailed into the yard, then said matter-of-factly, "Would you follow me, please, ladies and gentlemen?"

Of the motley group huddled in the snow there were only two other women, both attached to men who looked like husbands; Liane was the only woman on her own. She was glad in one way, for the last thing she felt like was company and small talk, and most certainly she could not share her fear with anyone. Yet, as she followed four or five of the others into the front door of the school, she felt very much alone.

The school was warm, and smelled as schools always did, of chalk and damp rubber boots and floor wax. The policeman led them into an auditorium with a tiled floor and a stage, flipped on the lights, waited until they were all gathered there, then said, "A farmer just up the road should be along shortly with something hot to eat... if you could see your way to pay him a small amount, I'm sure it would be appreciated. There are bedrolls in the furthest classroom down the hall, and blankets in the closet there. And we ask you not to smoke inside, please."

"Sounds like this has happened before," said the more jovial-looking husband.

"Every year, sir, at least once," said the policeman with a grin. "This is a bad stretch of highway. No one else will be joining you, because we also closed off the road behind you a few miles back. You should be able to get on your way by daylight tomorrow, say seven or so...one of us will be here to advise you." He paused inquiringly. "Any questions?"

Trying to keep her voice level, Liane asked, "Is there a telephone I can use?"

"There's a pay phone down the hall, ma'am. Oh, and the toilets are to the right. Anything else?" He waited a moment, then saluted them with a cheery smile and left the auditorium, his boots clicking on the tiles.

The jovial man took charge. "Why don't we go around the group with first names," he suggested, "seeing as how we're going to spend the night together? I'm Joe and this is my wife, Mabel."

Mabel smiled self-consciously, plucking at the buttons on her plain wool coat. Liane said her name in turn. The driver of the Chevrolet, who had his eye on her already and would have to be handled firmly, was called Henry, while the undistinguished man who had parked next to her mumbled something that sounded like Chester. The owner of the red wagon, who proved to be just as attractive under fluorescent light as outdoors, and who did not look as though he wanted to be within ten feet of her, was named Jake.

Jake. The name suited him, she decided caustically. A very masculine name, brief and uncompromising.

Not that it mattered to her what his name was.

She excused herself and found the telephone, fumbling for a coin in her wallet. The phone was in working order; with a silent prayer of gratitude, she dialed the number, and waited for someone to answer.

"Hello?"

"Megan? It's Liane."

"I'm *so* glad to hear from you; I was worried about you. We've got a foot of snow already, and more to come; why is it that the storms that aren't forecast are always the worst ones—are you all right?"

Pauses when Megan stopped for breath always had to be seized. "I'm spending the night in a school in the Wentworth Valley," Liane said. "Megan——"

"How romantic! Any tall, dark strangers?"

"No," said Liane, remembering how Jake's hair had shone black as a raven's wing under the fluorescent lights. "Megan, will you keep a close eye on Patrick for me? Don't let him——"

"What a worrywart you are," Megan interrupted fondly. "I always keep an eye on him, you know that; we're playing checkers right now, and as usual he's beating me. He says he gets his brains from his mother, which hardly seems fair when you're so beautiful as well... What did you say?"

"I said may I speak to him?" Liane put in, feeling her lips curve in a smile. It was hard to feel terrified when talking to Megan.

"Of course you can... Patrick, it's your mother."

The receiver changed hands. "I've got four crowns already," said Patrick. "Megan's only got one."

Liane swallowed hard, suddenly overcome by the sound of his voice, so well-known, so well-loved. Patrick was her vulnerable point, the chink in her armor; and how shrewdly her father had divined that.

"You there, Mom?"

"Yes, darling, I'm here... Patrick, I won't be home until tomorrow; I'm stuck in a schoolhouse because of the storm——"

"We got the afternoon off school, and me and Clancy made a launching pad in the snow for our rocket."

Patrick's present career plan was to be an astronaut. Liane said carefully, "Patrick, don't speak to any strangers, will you? Or take a ride from anyone you don't know."

"You've told me all that stuff trillions of times, Mom."

"Well, I'm telling you again," she said, and heard the unaccustomed sharpness in her voice.

Patrick heard it, too. "Okay," he agreed, sounding subdued.

"It's important, Patrick," she insisted. "I'll explain when I get home. What are you having for supper?"

"Tacos with jalapeño peppers," he said enthusiastically, and began to describe the cookies Megan had made that afternoon.

Someone had carved a set of initials in the doorframe by the telephone; Liane traced them with her fingernail, not noticing the man who had come out of the auditorium to stand in the hallway only a few feet away from her. "Darling," she said finally, "I've got to go; someone else might want the phone. Take care of yourself, won't you? And remember what I said... I love you, Patrick."

"Me too," replied Patrick, his standard reply ever since he had stopped being one of the little kids at primary school.

Liane hung up, and for a moment rested her forehead on the cold blue metal of the telephone. He would be all right until she got home. Of course he would be. Her father didn't know where she and Patrick lived. She had to hold on to that fact, and stop panicking.

"I'd like to use the telephone, if you don't mind."

Liane jumped, knocking the receiver off the hook so that it banged against the wall; she had thought she was alone. Knowing who she was going to see, because she had recognized the voice, she slowly put the receiver back, trying to calm the inner trembling that had been with her ever since her father's ultimatum. Only when she thought she had herself under control did she turn.

Jake was standing not twenty feet from her. The hall was brightly lit, and she saw no reason to amend her initial impression that he was the most attractive man she had ever seen. Yet, despite the bright lights, she thought of him instantly as a man of darkness. Thoughtfully she let her eyes rove over him. Was it the jet black hair, a little too long for current fashion? The deep-set eyes, so dark as to seem black as well? Or the faint stubble of beard, black against his tanned skin? Even his tan was too dark for a Canadian winter.

It was none of those things, she decided. It had more to do with his stillness as he waited—the stillness of the hunter waiting for its prey, and with the guardedness of his eyes—eyes that could keep any number of secrets, and keep them well. His height, the breadth of his shoulders, she saw and dismissed. It was the paradoxical blend of looseness and tension in his body that held her attention. He was, she was quite sure, in superb condition.

"The telephone," he repeated with rather overdone patience.

Liane flushed, aware that she had been staring at him in a way she never ordinarily stared at a man. But if she had been staring at him, so had he at her. He would have seen her rose pink jacket, she thought, and the matching angora sweater, its neckline hugging her throat, her pencil-slim gray skirt and polished brown boots, the soft fall of her blond hair over her collar. These were obvious to any observer. But would he have discerned the wariness in her blue eyes, the withholding that so often characterized her dealings with the opposite sex? And would he pick up the anxiety that was shivering along every nerve in her body?

She said, holding his gaze with her own, and not allowing even a trace of sarcasm to show in her voice, "Thank you for waiting."

He took a couple of paces toward her. "You get under my skin, you know that?"

"You make it fairly obvious."

"I'm not usually so lacking in subtlety."

"I'm sure you're not," she retorted dryly.

"It's not just that you're beautiful," he said in a voice without a trace of emotion. "Lots of men must have told you that, and I never did like being one of the crowd." He paused, scrutinizing her as if she were a specimen on a tray. "You look so goddamn fragile with those big blue eyes of yours...you've got that air of helpless, appealing femininity down to a fine art, haven't you? Most men fall for it, of course—I'm sure it's a very valuable commodity."

Her eyes sparking with fury, Liane snapped, "Are you implying that I'm trying to attract *your* attention?"

"Not necessarily mine."

"Oh, so any man will do?" She gave a sudden snort of laughter. "I hate to ruin your theory, but you're way off base." Then she paused, raising her brows with gentle irony. "For someone who was in a hurry for the phone, you're spending rather a lot of time talking to a woman it's clear you detest. Are you sure you're not trying to attract *my* attention?"

"Who's Patrick?" Jake said abruptly.

Liane paled, her voice like a whiplash. "How do you know about Patrick?"

The dark eyes gleamed at her quizzically. "You told him you loved him not two minutes ago."

"Oh...of course." Liane rubbed her forehead with fingers that were unsteady, realizing once again how deeply off balance she was. She said flatly, "Patrick is not, and never will be, any concern of yours."

"That's quite an act—the trembling fingers, the pale cheeks...very clever."

With total honesty, and with the flood of energy that such honesty usually brought, Liane said, "I don't like you! I don't like you at all."

"So perhaps we'd better agree on mutual dislike, and stay out of each other's way for the next twelve hours?"

"That seems like a fine idea to me," Liane agreed vigorously. "The smartest thing you've said so far."

Jake took another few steps toward her, close enough for her to see that his hair was shiningly clean, curling around his ears. Well-shaped ears, Liane thought, she who never normally noticed a man's ears. "So you don't think I'm very smart?" he said smoothly.

Suddenly wishing Mabel or Chester or even Henry would appear, Liane replied, "You've stereotyped me from the first minute you saw me—admit it! The helpless little woman, the typical dumb blonde."

He favored her with a wolfish grin. "Not quite typical, my dear."

She didn't know which infuriated her more—his smile or his endearment. She did realize that her hands were no longer trembling and that her nerves seemed to have settled down. So unwittingly he was doing her a favor, this black-haired man who hated blondes. And how often, she thought wryly, did one have the chance to be as blatantly rude as she was about to be? She said crisply, "Let's get a couple of things straight. I was born female with blond hair and blue eyes, and my genes dictated that I stopped growing at five-foot-five—not much I can do about any of that. So if you have a problem with the way I look, that's *your* problem. Not mine. Secondly, I hope that when you deign to favor a woman with your attention you choose a redhead or a brunette. For her sake, poor thing." She smiled at him sweetly. "Now perhaps you'd better make your phone call...you wouldn't want to keep her waiting, would you?"

His grin this time was frankly appreciative. "Did I say helpless? I take it back. You're as helpless as a barracuda."

If she had thought him attractive before, his smile made him nigh on irresistible. Which, Liane thought crossly, he no doubt knew. It was time—past time—she got out of here. She said coldly, "We're descending to the level of childish insult," and stalked past him.

Or at least that was her plan. But Jake, in a gesture so swift that she didn't even see it, grabbed her by the sleeve of her jacket and said, "Trading insults is rather exhilarating, wouldn't you agree? If we'd met at a cocktail party we'd be making civilized small talk, and we'd both be bored to tears."

Liane was not sure it would be possible to be bored in the same room with this man, although she was not about to tell him that. "Trading insults would pall just as quickly," she asserted, and reached down to pluck his hand from her sleeve.

His fingers were warm and lean and very strong, gripping her jacket tenaciously. Her own looked slim and—yes—very feminine resting over his. She said sharply, "Please let go."

"When I'm ready."

Any pleasure in the exchange was gone. Drawing on every ounce of her self-control, Liane told him evenly, "You have two choices. You can let go, or I'll scream my head off, which will bring Joe, Chester and the rest to the rescue, and surely cause you at least minimal embarrassment."

Jake dropped her arm immediately, his eyes trained on her face. "Three choices," he said. "I could have prevented you from screaming."

Liane felt a shudder of animal fear course along her nerves. Jake could have prevented her, she was sure of it. Her mind flinching from the means he might have used, she stepped back and said with as much dignity as she could muster, "I don't want anything more to do with you—so kindly stay away from me."

"My pleasure," he responded with another of those predatory smiles.

Wishing she could have had the last word, Liane turned on her heel and hurried back toward the auditorium. The girls' toilet was just beyond it; she went inside, hearing the door swing shut behind her, and thankfully found herself alone. The mirror over one of the institutional white sinks showed her blue eyes that were undoubtedly big, and a bone-structure undeniably fragile. She also looked exhausted.

After seven o'clock tomorrow morning she would never need see Jake again. Drawing several deep breaths, something she always found calming, she washed her hands with the strong-smelling liquid green soap and dried them on a paper towel. Then she went back to the auditorium.

In her absence Joe and two of the other men had set up long tables along the wall, and through the door at the far end a couple of men were carrying large aluminum saucepans. Liane went to help, and was sent to the staffroom for bowls and cutlery. The activity was soothing, and, when they all gathered several minutes later around one of the tables for soup and sandwiches, there was definitely the air of a picnic. The soup— chicken and vegetable—was delicious, Jake was sitting at the far end of the table from Liane, and she had not eaten since breakfast. She began eating, chatting to Mabel on one side and being careful not to be too friendly to Henry on her other.

Her enjoyment was augmented when she heard Jake mention that all the airports in Nova Scotia and Prince Edward Island were closed. So her father's hands were tied; he could do nothing while the storm lasted. Patrick was, for now, safe. The other thing she learned during the meal was that Jake was on his way back to Ottawa, having been visiting friends in Halifax. Ottawa was hundreds of miles from the little village of Hilldale in

Prince Edward Island. Just as well, she thought, and accepted another helping of soup.

After the meal, in which they demolished mounds of sandwiches as well as three raisin pies, Liane helped clean up the dishes while the men dragged in bedrolls and arranged them on the floor. An impromptu card game then started. Liane joined in; she had an excellent memory and a mathematical sense of the odds of playing a certain card, both of which she had bequeathed to her son. The contest started mildly enough with hearts, then moved to poker. As the pile of pennies accumulated in front of her, Liane was aware of Jake watching her, his expression inscrutable.

That would show him, she thought wickedly. Dumb blonde, indeed!

By eleven o'clock everyone was settling down for the night, sharing what blankets they had. Liane had elected to stay in her clothes, because she had not brought a housecoat and her nightgown was made of pale blue satin, which did not seem very appropriate for the floor of an auditorium. Not to mention Henry, who had already made several heavy-handed and suggestive remarks in the course of the card game.

She used her jacket as a pillow, and wrapped the rather musty blanket that Joe had found in one of the cupboards around her legs. The only light came from the tall poles outside the school. Closing her eyes, and blanking her father, Patrick, and Jake from her mind, Liane fell asleep.

CHAPTER TWO

IT WAS dark when Liane woke. Her legs were cold, and her neck cramped by the bulk of her jacket; Joe, on her right side, was snoring energetically. She lay still, remembering all that had happened the day before, wondering if it was still snowing, already worrying whether the ferries would be running.

They had to be, she thought. She had to get home.

Money can do anything, Liane. Money can do anything at all.

Clenching her fingers into fists, she closed her eyes again, desperate for the oblivion that sleep brought. But she could not shut out her father's voice any more than she could control the black thoughts that the middle of the night could foster so easily.

Her father wanted Patrick.

Her father was a rich man, used to getting his own way, used to buying people as easily as if they were the possessions with which he surrounded himself. He would not allow his daughter, his only remaining child, to thwart him. Sooner or later he would find out that she and Patrick lived by the Hillsborough River on an estate that belonged to Alma and George Forster. And then what would he do?

He would take Patrick. She knew he would. He had as much as said he would.

What in God's name could she do?

She spread her jacket over her feet and rested her cheek on her arm, staring into the darkness, feeling more alone than she ever had in her life. She had to fight. With

every weapon at her command she had to try to outwit
Murray Hutchins. Because Patrick deserved better than
the kind of upbringing she had had.

But her father had money. He could hire lawyers to
blacken her character, make her seem an unfit mother
for a young boy—that was one of the threats he had
hurled at her yesterday after he had lost his temper with
her. He had a great deal of money, and the power that
money brought. She had neither.

Liane turned over on her other side, pulling the blanket
to her chin. Resolutely she closed her eyes, determined
to sleep, for she would need all her strength for the day
ahead. But her shoulders began to itch in the angora
sweater, while her toes, despite her jacket, remained ice
cold. And she was thirsty.

Against her will, her thoughts marched on. The worst
thing about yesterday's visit was not that she had instigated it herself, but that she had been reduced to the
status of a child again. She was twenty-seven years old,
and in the eight years since she had fled her father's
house she had borne a son and made a way in the world
for the two of them. Yet three-quarters of an hour with
Murray Hutchins had pushed those years aside. She had
felt like a five-year-old, his fierce blue eyes and gravelly
voice awakening memories of long-ago rages for mis-
demeanors she had since forgotten.

She had hated feeling like that terrified little girl.

Liane curled her toes into the warmth of her jacket.
For ten more interminable minutes she wooed sleep,
during which time Joe stopped snoring, Henry started,
and a snowplow rattled past the school, turned around
and rattled back again. She waited two or three more
minutes to see if anyone else had woken up, then very
quietly got out of bed. Padding on her stockinged feet
out of the auditorium, she went to the toilet, where she

splashed cold water on her face and drank deeply from the tap.

She was wide-awake. Leaving the toilet, she crept down the hallway to the furthest classroom, which was decorated with colored cutouts of snowmen and skiers, and whose desks obviously belonged to very small children. Obscurely comforted by the clutter, which reminded her of Patrick's bedroom in the loft at home, Liane perched herself on top of the desk nearest the window, rested her elbows on her knees, and gazed out into the darkness.

A few tiny snowflakes were drifting past the rectangular panes. The radiators gurgled and groaned. Otherwise the world was silent, and she alone in it. Alone, and not knowing what to do.

She tried to think, to assess her options logically. She could stay in the house she and Patrick had shared for the last three years, and assume her father would not have the nerve to kidnap his only grandchild. She could hire a lawyer, lay the whole story in front of him and count on the law to protect her. Or she could leave the house and go into hiding...but where, and how? Patrick had to go to school and she had to work, so how could she hide? Besides which Patrick loved living in their wing of the big brick house, and needed the stability of the life Liane had been able to build for him. For Patrick had no father of his own...

There was very little she could do, Liane thought, feeling panic nibble at her control. Her father held all the high cards; her hand was virtually worthless.

But if she did nothing her father would take Patrick. He had always taken what he wanted.

Around and around her thoughts chased each other. She could move to Toronto and lose herself among the crowds; but she could not afford to live in Toronto. She could move in with Megan, Fitz, and the boys, but she could not stay there forever, and her father could afford to wait. She could get a very large dog and leave it loose to wander the grounds.

That seemed the best idea yet. Greatly cheered by a mental image of her father being chased by a slavering Great Dane, she gazed out of the window, and in the reflection she saw someone move into the doorway behind her.

Stifling a shriek of alarm, Liane swiveled on the desk and saw that it was Henry. Not Jake. Not sure whether she was relieved or disappointed, and not wanting to dwell on either of these responses, she pulled her skirt down over her knees and said, "The snowplow woke me—but I was just about to go back to bed."

Henry was somewhat overweight, and rolled from side to side like a dory on a swell as he navigated the aisle between the desks, ending up too close to Liane for her own comfort. He said breezily, "You look as though you've got the cares of the world on your shoulders—a pretty little thing like you... what's the trouble—hubby pulling a fast one on you?"

Were life so simple... Liane thought ironically. A wandering husband she could cope with. She said coldly, "I don't have a husband," and slid down from the desk.

It was a tactical error. Henry loomed over her. "No husband, eh?" he said with a laugh that was meant to be convivial and sounded merely coarse. "Then I can fix what's ailing you." He reached for her with a hand like a bear's paw.

Liane was young and agile. She ducked, slid between two desks and, with her knee, shoved one of them in Henry's way. "I do not need fixing, as you so crudely phrase it," she seethed. "Neither do I need a husband, thank you very much. And if you so much as put a hand on me I'll smash this desk over your head!"

In an injured voice Henry said, "Now that's no way——"

From the doorway someone laughed, a deep belly laugh of genuine appreciation. "I think she means it, Henry," Jake said. "If I were you, I'd go back to bed."

Laughter still lingered on his words. Nevertheless, Henry, after muttering something very rude under his breath, made a beeline for the door. Jake stood aside with a mocking grin, and watched Henry's no doubt rapid progress down the hall. Then he said to Liane, "A midnight tryst? Did you think the better of it when the time came to deliver?"

Liane replied trenchantly, "I wouldn't have expected *you* to interpret that charming little scene in any other way—it would have to be me who lured him in here with my big blue eyes, wouldn't it? It couldn't possibly be the man who was at fault."

Jake sauntered into the room, his hands in the pockets of his well-cut pants bulky wool sweater making his shoulders look broader than they were. "Henry's a wealthy man, and recently widowed. He surely shared that little snippet of information with you?"

"I didn't give him time," Liane replied pithily. "And, believe me, wealth would not recommend him to me." She put her head to one side, fluttered her lashes, which were long and thick and one of her better points, and discovered to her surprise that she was enjoying herself. "So, besides being a helpless clinging vine, I'm also a ruthless gold digger? Quite a combination."

"Money is a very useful commodity."

"Indeed it is. But not so useful that I would contemplate even for a moment allowing the likes of Henry to maul me."

"Bigger game in mind?" asked Jake.

He was standing with one row of desks between her and him. Plenty close, thought Liane, watching the shadows slant across his face. "The only game I play is poker," she said.

"And that extremely well." He stepped over the desks so that he was between her and the door. "A poker face is a bit of a cliché, isn't it? Yet you've obviously trained yourself to keep your thoughts hidden…I wonder why?"

Struggling very hard to maintain the inscrutability he was describing, Liane suggested pleasantly, "To keep men as inquisitive as you guessing, perhaps?"

He gave a reluctant smile. "You have an answer for everything, don't you? So if you didn't entice Henry in here with dalliance in mind, why *are* you gazing out of the window at a view that's less than inspiring at——" he checked his watch "—three in the morning? Anyone with a clear conscience would surely be asleep."

"So what's on your conscience, Jake?"

This time he laughed outright. "I left myself wide open for that one, didn't I? I saw you leave the auditorium, and then a few minutes later I saw Henry go after you… Put it down to simple curiosity."

"I don't think anything's simple with you," Liane said, and wondered where that knowledge came from.

Jake said very softly, "You're a witch, do you know that?"

She took a deep breath, not sure she could trust herself to speak. If she was a witch he was the demon king, she thought fancifully, with his black hair and his black eyes and the sheer power of his presence. For she was aware of him through every pore in her body, in a way she did not care for at all. In a way that was both unique and frightening. She said steadily, feeling the edge of the desk press against the back of her thighs, "I'm neither witch nor gold digger, nor clinging vine, Jake. Just an ordinary woman. That's all."

His eyes trained on her face, he observed, "An ordinary woman who happens to be scared out of her wits—what are you so afraid of, Liane?"

"I'm not!" Involuntarily she moved back; the legs of the desk scraped on the floor.

"Yes, you are. You have been ever since you talked to the police officer who was directing the traffic yesterday. What have you done to make you so afraid?"

"Oh, it would have to be something I've done, wouldn't it?" she said bitterly. "That's the way your mind works."

"That's right . . . so who are you running from? Why don't you tell me? Maybe I can help."

For a wild moment she was tempted to pour out all her troubles, to see if indeed there was some way he could help; for she needed help—she knew that. She could not fight her father alone; she had never been able to. Swallowing hard, she told him in a stony voice, "Your imagination's working overtime. I was upset because the roads were so bad; I've always hated driving in snow."

Jake said calmly, "You're lying."

Quite suddenly Liane lost her temper. In an exhilarating flood of energy she snapped, "Yes, I'm lying. Very clever of you, Jake, congratulations! What do you do for an encore?"

"This," he said, then took her in his arms, and kissed her.

It was a hard kiss, fueled by anger; it was also brief to the point of insult. Frozen by surprise, Liane stood stock-still as he released her, and said the first thing that came into her mind. "You use the same after-shave as my father."

"But not the same as Patrick?"

"Oh, no," she said, "not the same as Patrick."

She scowled at him, remembering the bite of his fingers through her sweater and the rasp of his beard on her chin. "You and Henry are birds of a feather—I'm not the slightest bit flattered by the attentions of either one of you."

She had known Jake would not like being bracketed with Henry; nor did he. She also knew a scathing retort was on the tip of his tongue, and braced herself. But instead he kept silent, regarding her unsmilingly, his mouth a forbidding line in a face carved to stillness. When she was sure she could not stand the silence a moment longer, he said in a voice from which any emotion had been removed, "I apologize for kissing you. I had no right to do that."

Liane's jaw dropped. "I have never in my life met anyone as disconcerting as you!" she exclaimed. "And that's the plain truth."

He gave her a crooked smile. "I believe you. So is my apology accepted?"

"Would it matter to you either way?"

"Enough that I'm asking."

She said slowly, "Yes, it's accepted."

"Good. Why were you so scared yesterday, Liane?"

In her stockinged feet Liane was considerably shorter than he. She gazed up at him, again visited by the urge to share the terror lurking in her heart like a coiled snake, yet at the same time knowing how impossible it was that she tell her story to a complete stranger. "I can't tell you, Jake," she said honestly. "I can't...I'm sorry."

In the dim light of the classroom her eyes were clear and candid. The man made a gesture of frustration that he halted in midair. "You don't trust me."

"How could I? I don't know you. And you've made it very clear you don't like me."

"Yeah..." For a minute he hesitated, as though considering what to do next. Then he said, clipping off the words, "You'd better go back to bed. I have a feeling the police are going to arrive at daybreak to hustle us out of here before school starts."

Liane felt a strange, and very strong, pang of loss. Tomorrow this dark-browed stranger would go his way

and she would go hers, and they would never meet again.
She was quite sure he didn't like her, equally sure he had
meant his offer of help. Perplexed, she murmured, "I
guess you're right...do you realize I don't even know
your last name?"

"Brande. Jacob Brande. Spelled with an 'e.'"

Seven years ago, when Patrick was born, Liane had
legally changed her surname to her mother's maiden
name. "Liane Daley," she replied formally.

"Miss?" he asked.

For Patrick's sake she went by Ms., which left open
the question of her marital status. "I've never been
married," she said.

"You must have been asked. Didn't any of them have
enough money?"

She replied inelegantly, "Stuff it, Jake—we women
aren't all gold diggers."

"Bed, Miss Daley."

She could have argued; she could have prolonged this
peculiar conversation in the middle of the night in a
country schoolhouse. But what was the point? Despite
the emotion that crackled between them, an emotion as
strong as it was negative, she and Jake had nothing to
say to each other. No shared past and no possible future.
Only a present, as inconclusive as it had been, oddly
enough, enlivening.

"Good night," she said, and found herself holding
out her hand.

Jake took it in his, pressed it firmly, and released it.
"Good night, Liane."

She had liked the strength of his grip, the smoothness
of his palm against hers. Unaware of how her features
were revealing her inner confusion, she turned away from
him and hurried down the aisle, her feet whispering on
the tiled floor.

The auditorium contained the same array of humped bodies, Henry with his back ostentatiously turned to her. Joe was snoring again. Liane lay down, fully intending to analyze what had transpired between her and Jake Brande, and woke to hear Mabel calling her name. "Time to get up, dear; the road's open and the storm's over... Did you have a good rest?"

Liane sat up, rubbing her eyes. She had been dreaming, one of those horrible dreams where you knew you could never run fast enough to escape your pursuer; she felt exactly like someone who had had five hours' sleep, and the prospect of the day ahead made her want to bury her head in her jacket and pretend the rest of the world did not exist. "Fine," she croaked.

"That's good," said Jake.

Liane winced. He was standing not ten feet from her, eyeing her sardonically. She blushed, wondering if he had been watching her sleep, wondering if the way he had kissed her was as fresh in his mind as it was in hers. She scrambled to her feet, showing rather a lot of leg as she did so, and pushed her hair back from her face, knowing from long experience that there would be blue shadows under her eyes, for her skin was too fair to hide the marks of a sleepless night. He, of course, looked fit and wide-awake, newly shaven, his hair gleaming under the lights. Not even a cut on his chin, she thought sourly. The man was inhuman.

She bent to get her toothbrush out of her overnight bag, and heard him say softly, for her ears alone, "A witch, a gold digger, and a grump in the mornings."

Aware that she was being thoroughly bitchy, and not in the least repentant, Liane retorted, "I hope you've never married, Jake Brande—think of the poor woman who'd have the gargantuan task of living up to you. Perfection is so difficult to emulate."

"So your tongue's just as sharp first thing in the morning," he observed amiably. "Why don't you go and wash your face? You'll both feel and look better."

There was a gleam of amusement in the black eyes. Liane fought back a smile, glad that her son was not here to listen to this undignified exchange—an exchange for which she would have chided him, and said ingenuously, "I could hardly feel worse—I've never been a morning person; I don't start to wake up for another two hours." Then, wondering what had possessed her to share this piece of rather personal information with a man who disliked her, she hurried to the toilets.

Hot water, a liberal application of makeup and a hairbrush made her look a great deal better. And Jake *had* called her beautiful. Wishing she could deal as easily with the knot of tension in her stomach as she could with her face, Liane went back to gather up her things. The bedrolls had been stashed away, and only a few of her fellow travelers were left.

Jake was nowhere to be seen.

Neither, on the plus side, was Henry.

Mabel bade her a hasty farewell. "Joe's in a hurry to get his first coffee of the day...fun, wasn't it, dear? Stay between the ditches, now." And she laughed heartily at her own wit.

Liane pulled on her jacket and zipped up her bag. Her car keys in her hand, she left the auditorium and headed outside. The cherry red wagon was gone.

He had not even said goodbye.

Her shoulders slumped, she unlocked her car. Before she could move she had to shovel behind the back wheels and clear off the front and back windows; her thin leather gloves and her boots were not improved by either task. Nor was her temper. He could at least have said goodbye. Or did he make a habit of kissing women at three in the morning—women he didn't even like? But, if he didn't like her, why was she so upset that he had left without bothering to speak to her?

He'd be adding feminine illogicality to her list of bad traits, she thought petulantly, slamming her door with unnecessary force.

Her own stormy blue eyes glared back at her in the rearview mirror. If Jake didn't like women, it was equally true that she didn't like men. She certainly didn't trust them. So what was all the fuss about?

It was an unanswerable question. Dimly aware that the inoffensive Chester was scraping the ice from his window a few feet away, she waved goodbye and backed out of her parking space. The sooner she got on the road and forgot about Jake Brande the better.

It was a beautiful day—the kind popularized by calendars and postcards. The sun was rising pale gold in a clear blue sky. The trees cast long purple shadows on the snow, where each branch was etched with the clarity of an Oriental print. The snow itself lay deep and smooth, simplifying the blinding whiteness of the landscape to a series of rounded curves.

Liane pulled onto the highway between tall banks of snow that the plow had left. Mabel and Joe were already out of sight. She moved up a gear, getting the feel of the road, which had been salted as well as plowed, and trying at the same time to settle her mind for the day ahead. She'd stop at a restaurant and get some coffee and toast, then she'd drive as fast as she could for the ferry.

The first restaurant she came to had a car she recognized as Joe's parked outside, but no red wagon. Liane kept going. The second restaurant, attached to a gas station, boasted a half-ton truck and a Cadillac. She could not—would not—pursue Jake any further. Her mouth set, Liane pulled in between the two vehicles and got out of her car. From the front seat of the Cadillac a primped little poodle wearing a pink satin bow on its collar barked at her hysterically. She made a horrible face at it and went inside.

Coffee and two very good homemade donuts made Liane feel much better. Half an hour later she was on her way again. She had to drive carefully because there were big patches of slush on the road, and she continually had to be washing the salt from her windshield; but the miles slowly accumulated, and by ten past nine she had left Nova Scotia and was taking the turnoff to the ferry. The countryside was now level and open, with farmhouses scattered here and there. The sun was convincingly warm through the car windows, and soon she would be home. Even the thought of her own four walls gave Liane confidence. She would figure out a way to deal with her father. Maybe she would have to alert all the neighbors, get a lawyer, and buy the Great Dane— all three strategies at once. Certainly she would have to tell Patrick what had transpired in his grandfather's house.

The miles ticked by. The road was flat and very straight, and her terror of the night before began to seem an exaggeration, exactly the kind of reaction her father had counted on. This time she wouldn't play, she thought fiercely. This time he had the wrong woman.

A bus roared toward her, slopping wet snow across the glass in front of her eyes. She blinked, turning on the wipers and watching the bus recede in her rearview mirror. Then her hands suddenly tightened on the wheel and the car swerved. There was a small red dot on the far horizon, following her.

Jake?

You're imagining things, Liane, she scolded herself. There are lots of red cars, any number of which could be heading for the ferry. A red vehicle does not have to belong to Jake. Anyway, Jake left ahead of you. Jake's probably halfway to Montreal by now.

The red dot was far enough behind that she could not distinguish whether it was a car or a wagon. Biting her lip, angry with herself that she could even care whether Jake was following her, she slackened her speed. She was climbing a long, gradual incline; once she was on the other side, and out of sight of the red vehicle, she'd slow right down and let it catch up.

Why, Liane? Why do you have to know whether it's Jake? What's Jake to you?

I'm interested, that's all. He's a very attractive man with whom—in one sense—I spent the night.

He didn't bother to say goodbye, though.

Scowling ferociously, Liane reached the top of the slope and started down the other side, and in a few moments the road behind her dropped out of sight. She then slipped back to third gear and coasted down the hill, feeling her heartbeat quicken in her breast and her knuckles whiten on the wheel.

With excruciating slowness the digital clock on her dashboard counted off the seconds. Then, in her rear-view mirror, she saw a cherry red wagon come over the hill. She would have recognized it anywhere. It was Jake's.

She speeded up again, and wondered if it was her imagination that the wagon had braked at the crest of the hill when the driver had seen her. And why was Jake coming to Prince Edward Island? In the summer, attracted by its miles of beaches, visitors inundated the island. But not in the winter. And last night he had told everyone he was on his way back to Ottawa.

He wants to see you again, Liane. That's why he didn't say goodbye.

Don't be silly! I outgrew Cinderella years ago.

She accelerated gradually. The wagon made no effort to catch up with her, maintaining the same distance between them. Realizing that she was smiling to herself, an idiotic smile she would have found difficult to erase or explain, Liane turned on the radio and began to sing along with Anne Murray's latest release.

The Northumberland Strait came into sight, its steel blue water patched with drift ice. When she reached Cape Tormentine, the red wagon pulled in at a gas station and parked by the pumps. Liane kept going, for where else would Jake be headed but for the ferry? She stopped at the toll booth, paid her ten dollars, and proceeded to the row of parked vehicles. Three other cars drove in behind her before the red wagon came into sight in her mirror and took its place in the line.

There was a twenty-minute wait for the next crossing. Liane stayed in her car, wondering what Jake would do.

He did nothing.

Ten minutes later the loudspeaker announced the boarding of the ferry, and the first vehicles started off for the loading ramps. Keeping her place in the line, Liane accelerated up the slope, then heard the hum of metal beneath her tires as she drove onto the upper deck of the boat. Obeying the traffic director, she parked in the inner lane. From experience she knew that drivers were not permitted to remain in their cars for the crossing; Jake would have to make a move. Checking her makeup in the mirror and smoothing on fresh lipstick, she wondered what he would say to her.

A dark blue car passed her, starting a new line of vehicles to her left. She instantly recognized the driver, for he too had spent the night in the school. Chester. A man as nondescript as his car.

With a pang of sheer terror Liane suddenly grabbed at the steering wheel, and the tube of lipstick fell into her lap. Jake behind her. Chester ahead of her. It could not be coincidence.

Either or both had been following her ever since she had left her father's yesterday afternoon. Either or both must be in her father's pay.

What a fool she had been! It was totally logical that her father would have her followed. It was the obvious thing for him to do, because it was by far the easiest way for him to find out where she was living. Keep a safe distance behind her and let her lead them to the place she called home. Let her betray her own whereabouts—her father would like that. And also, of course, the whereabouts of Patrick, the place he too called home.

She had almost fallen into the trap.

Either or both, she thought numbly. Jake in her father's pay? Or Chester? Or both? How could she know?

She couldn't.

She couldn't trust either one.

CHAPTER THREE

CHESTER was getting out of his car, hunching his neck into the collar of his coat against the wind that was whistling across the open deck. Or was that his motive? Liane wondered, watching him with wide eyes. Maybe he was hunching down to hide from her. The traffic warden had inadvertently made him park in a place she could scarcely fail to see him, so now he was doing his best to be unobtrusive.

Was that why Jake had made no effort to catch up with her, or to talk to her in the ferry parking lot? He didn't need to. He had her in his sights, he knew where she would be for the next hour. He therefore had no need to talk to her.

For much the same reasons he had not needed to say goodbye to her at the school this morning.

To the tension lying like a lump of stone in her belly she now added pain. For she and Jake had connected. Something—an emotional charge, an attraction neither had been willing to acknowledge, let alone act upon—had happened between them. Something real. And now she was faced with the very strong possibility that Jake was in her father's pay.

As her thoughts carried her inexorably forward, Liane slumped down further in her seat, wondering if she could get away with disobeying the injunction to leave her car. Jake seemed a much more likely suspect than Chester. For Jake was dangerous—she had recognized that immediately. Far more dangerous than the inoffensive Chester. Had Jake not wanted her to scream last night, she would not have screamed; and he would not have been fussy about his methods.

The traffic director tapped on her window, his bright orange jacket flapping in the wind. "We ask the passengers not to stay in their vehicles, please, miss," he said.

He looked large and solid and safe. She wondered what he would say were she to tell him why she wanted to stay in her car. He'd probably have her committed for paranoid delusions, she thought wryly, and smiled up at him. "I'll be right out," she said.

She picked up her lipstick, put it back in her purse, pulled on her gloves, and got out of the car. Although the wind was bitingly cold, keen with the knife-sharp tang of the sea, she walked over to the railing and stood there for a moment, watching the slush of ice particles undulate on the swell, the lamenting of the gray and white gulls like a dirge in her ears. What was she going to do? She could not possibly drive straight home, leading Chester and Jake to the place where she lived. Leading them to Patrick.

The engines began to rumble and the deck shook as if it had the ague, as, in a swirl of foam, the ferry edged away from the dock. Gulls rose, screeching, from the breakwater. The wind sliced through Liane's jacket and reddened her cheeks. What she could not do, she decided ruefully, was stay on deck for the next forty-five minutes.

She went downstairs and joined the lineup at the snack bar, ordering a muffin, an egg and coffee. When she had paid for the food, she picked up her tray. Jake was sitting at a window table. He raised a hand in casual salute, and indicated the empty seat across from him.

It was his very casualness that angered Liane the most. She shot him a fulminating glance, and carried the tray to a booth on the opposite side of the room. Chester was nowhere in sight.

The window was streaked with salt; through it she watched the shoreline recede as she munched on her muffin.

An all-too-familiar voice remarked, "It's past ten o'clock—or are you a grump until noon?" Then, without asking her permission, Jake sat down opposite her.

Although his voice had had a trace of amusement in it, his eyes had none. His eyes, which had seemed black in the middle of the night, were actually a very dark brown, the peat brown of a bog, full of unknown depths and hidden dangers. Liane said evenly, "Jake, I don't want to sit with you. Will you please leave?"

"What's happened between three in the morning and now?" he asked. "You weren't in any hurry to get rid of me then."

She looked at him in silence, seeing other details that had escaped her in the half light. His lashes were as long as hers, and as black as his hair; there was a small white scar over one cheekbone. She had thought him honest, she realized painfully. Honest in his dislike of her, honest in the sparring they had indulged in. But it had not been honest at all. He was her father's henchman. And as if to emphasize the distance between them, to her nostrils drifted the scent of his after-shave.

"Say something, Liane—because you're still running scared, I can tell."

That he should openly allude to a fear whose cause he knew very well, and was contributing to, filled her with ice-cold rage. Yet could she afford to let him know that she had guessed why he was following her? That she was wise to his game? Poker face, she warned herself. Better to lie low rather than alert him that she would be using every ounce of her intelligence to evade him once they were off the ferry. With an almost superhuman effort she swallowed her rage and said with cool precision, "I thought you were very rude to leave the school without saying goodbye. I place a high premium on good manners."

Jake leaned back in his seat. "I knew I'd be seeing you again."

Every sense alert, Liane regarded him through narrowed eyes. Was he about to throw his hand openly on the table? "And how did you know that?"

His smile was lazy, full of assurance. "You need help. I've got some spare time—I don't have to be back in Ottawa right away. So I followed you."

"You weren't behind me when I stopped for coffee," she flashed.

"You've got a PEI licence plate, and you told the police officer last night you had to get back to the island. I didn't have to be Sherlock Holmes to figure out where you were headed."

"I don't want your help," she said.

"I know you don't. But I don't like seeing people frightened to the extent you——"

"Chivalry went out several centuries ago," she interrupted, allowing some of her fury to surface. "As did knights in shining armor. I can look after my own life, Jake. I don't need a man to do it for me."

"Why is it," he remarked, "that every time I come within ten feet of you I want to kiss you?"

Across the room a child started to cry; with a loud clatter someone dropped a plate at the food counter. Liane remembered that brief kiss of the night before, the unexpected warmth of his lips, the shock and heat that had chased each other through her body, and said in a choked voice, "Unless you want half a fried egg dumped on your head, don't even contemplate kissing me again."

"I didn't say I was going to kiss you, I only said I wanted to. And I'll fantasize if I please. What I'd really like to know is why *you're* the one to set me off...I don't even like blondes."

"You don't like women!"

"You have a point there," Jake drawled. "So why you?"

Because my father is a very rich man? The words were on the tip of Liane's tongue; she bit them back, gave him a leisurely survey, and said, "You're not bad looking, Jake, and despite the feminist movement there are a lot of women around who seem to think a man will solve all their problems—perhaps you're just not used to females who don't fall flat on their backs at the first glance from you...I, however, will admit to finding your techniques a trifle heavy-handed."

She smiled at him placidly and took the last bite of muffin. He had not liked her little speech, she could tell; in fact, if looks could kill, she would be slithering to the floor of the cafeteria right now. But when she thought of Patrick she could not dredge up even a twinge of repentance.

"Given the opportunity," Jake said silkily, "I'm sure I could change your mind as to my—er—technique."

"I'm not going to waste any chips on that particular hand."

"I can see that there was too much talk last night and not enough action." He pushed himself up from the bench, so that momentarily he towered over her, and she was forced to crane her neck back to meet his eyes. He was, she saw, extremely angry. "I won't make the same mistake again."

"Not with me you won't," she answered cordially. Then she directed her most dazzling smile at him, for she had just thought of how she would get rid of both him and Chester on the way to Charlottetown. It was a

very simple plan, and, as with most simple plans, she
was almost sure it would work.

"You haven't seen the last of me, Liane," Jake said
levelly, then turned on his heel and left. He was wearing
a very expensive leather jacket over his sweater. Her
father must pay well, she thought bitterly, and took a
gulp of coffee. It was lukewarm. She made a face, and
tried to forget the undeniable menace in Jake's parting
statement by concentrating on her plan. All she had to
do was find a pay phone once she was off the ferry, and
pray that her friend Percy was home.

She finished her coffee, wandered through the lounge,
where Chester was curled up in a corner seat with his
eyes closed, and Jake was reading a magazine, and went
out on deck. The wind was still ice cold. But it was clean
and it was honest, thought Liane, taking a deep breath
as it whipped her hair around her ears. Chester on one
side of the lounge, and Jake on the other—how she
loathed them for their duplicity and their greed!

She found a corner near the bridge where she was
sheltered from the wind and where the white-painted
bulwarks reflected the sun, and leaned back, closing her
eyes. If her plan with Percy worked, she would be as
safe as it was possible for her to be, because she was not
in the phone book and she could not be traced through
her license-plate numbers. She would have bought time.
Time to come up with a strategy to outwit her father.

The sun was warm on her face and the engines
grumbled in a comforting rhythm. When next she opened
her eyes, the red cliffs of the island she had called home
since before Patrick was born were close to the boat.
Red cliffs capped with white snow under an achingly
blue sky—another postcard scene, she thought, and went
below to sit in her car because she did not want to talk
to Jake again.

In her car she kept the windows rolled up, and locked her doors, staring straight ahead as Chester walked past her. The ferry bumped against the dock, and the ramp creaked down on its pulleys. The first cars drove off. Liane followed, watching for a pay phone as she drove into the little town of Borden. When she saw one at a gas station, she pulled out of the line of traffic, parked in front of the phone, and inserted her money in the slot with fingers that felt clumsy with nervousness. Willing Percy to be home, she rang his number.

"Hello there," Percy bellowed.

Percy, who had perfect hearing, operated on the principle that the rest of the world was deaf. "It's Liane," she answered in a moderate voice. "Percy, will you do me a favor?"

"Was thinking about you yesterday...Rosie had twins and I figured your Patrick might like to see 'em."

Rosie was a very large Holstein. "I'm sure he would," Liane said, and from the corner of her eye saw Jake draw up at the opposite end of the tarmac and park, making no attempt to disguise his presence. "Percy, I need a favor and I can't explain what it's all about right now. I've just got off the ferry—in about twenty minutes I'll be driving past your place, and I'm being followed by a bright red wagon and a small dark blue car—I think it's a Honda... Will you let me pass and then drive your manure spreader across the road and pretend it's broken down? The longer you can delay them, the better."

Percy gave an astonished snort of laughter. "You've been watching too much TV, girl! Sure I'll do it—be a change from workin' in the barn. If you get ten minutes or so, that be enough?"

"More than enough. Bless you, Percy...I'll explain in a couple of days."

"You do that—and bring your boy with you." Percy gave another uncouth snort. "I got some real ripe pig manure; that'll fix 'em."

Chester's blue car slowed fractionally as it passed the gas station, then kept going. "I've got to go," Liane said, her mouth suddenly dry. "Thanks a million, Percy. Bye."

She got back in her car and edged into the line of traffic again. Two blocks farther on she saw the dark blue Honda tucked into the parking lot of a bank; had she not been looking for it, she would have missed it. So it was the two of them, she thought, and swallowed hard. Jake alone was a formidable opponent, without adding Chester as well.

As she left the town and headed inland the traffic gradually thinned, until Jake was four cars back and Chester three behind him. Very carefully Liane tried to increase the gap without being too obvious about it, grateful that the highway had been so well plowed. Although one of the cars between her and Jake pulled off at a restaurant, and a few minutes later another took the turnoff to Victoria, Jake seemed content at the distance between them, making no effort to close it. And Chester, of course, would follow Jake.

Aware that under all her other concerns she was burningly angry with her father for subjecting her to this ridiculous chase, Liane drove on. The gentle hills and snow-filled valleys, the tidy farms with their dark green woodlots passed her one by one, all familiar, all somehow increasing her rage at her father—and therefore at Jake and Chester—that her home, her place of sanctuary, was no longer inviolate.

She checked her watch, knowing that in five minutes she would reach the sprawling acreage on both sides of the road that had been in Percy's family for over two hundred years. On the next straight stretch the black car

between her and Jake passed her, leaving only a small
truck in sight apart from her two pursuers. Mentally
apologizing to the driver of the truck for the delay she
would be causing him, she drove up the last hill before
Percy's, her fingers tense on the wheel.

As soon as she came in sight, a green tractor pulling
a long red manure spreader lurched onto the road. It
was Percy's largest tractor. Liane put her foot to the
floor, surged past him and waved her gloved hand,
grinning widely. Percy waved back, crossed her lane with
the tractor, and stopped. The tractor was nearly in the
ditch, while the spreader, which indeed smelled very ripe,
had its back end in the driveway. The road was completely blocked. Liane waved again, and speeded up. This
was her chance. She must take full advantage of it.

She kept on the same road at the first set of cross-
roads, but at the second, having first checked in her
mirror that she was not being followed, she turned left.
Then she took a series of right and left turns, staying
both north and west of the city of Charlottetown,
glancing nervously in her mirror at every turn. Although
for a few miles a battered old Jeep followed her, then a
shiny green sedan, there was no sign of either a red wagon
or a small dark blue car.

She had won. With Percy's help she had duped Jake
and Chester, and had, at least temporarily, defeated her
father as well.

Beginning to relax, Liane went north again, and only
when she was well away from the city did she turn back
toward the river. It was the most circuitous route she
had ever taken to get home. But it had worked. She
would not be seeing Jake or Chester again.

Chester she could not have cared less about. Jake she
did.

Scowling to herself, she topped a hill and saw below
her the wide valley of the Hillsborough River, a river

that nearly divided the province in two. She would soon be home.

Eight years ago, three months pregnant, Liane had run from Murray Hutchins and from all that he represented, settling in a new province that had a wide stretch of water between her and him. Supporting herself with the money her mother had left her, she had given birth to her son, and had begun to make new friends.

When Patrick turned two, she had started taking courses in landscape design, and when her mother's money had run out she'd worked in the summers for nurseries and in the winters at the local library. Three years ago, through her friends Megan and Fitz Donleavy, she had met the Forsters, an elderly couple who summered on the island and spent the rest of the year in Florida; they were looking for someone to care for their gardens in summer and the greenhouse and conservatory in the winters. For Liane the job could not have been better, for she could live in one wing of the house with her son, work on the premises all summer, and still keep her position at the library.

The Forsters were away at the moment. She and Patrick were alone in the big house on the banks of the river, a fact that until yesterday had never worried her at all. Megan and Fitz lived a mile away in the village of Hilldale; a mile was not far, she told herself firmly, and took the turnoff to the estate.

The Forsters owned the better part of three hundred acres, with formal gardens around the gracious brick house, merging into carefully tended woods which in the spring were a blaze of color from azaleas and rhododendrons, and which opened out into a field of wildflowers that led down to the river. Liane had loved the property from the first moment she had seen it, had felt her spirits expand and her soul heal as she worked on the grounds, and had soon seen how much happier Patrick was here than in the city.

I won't leave here, she vowed, parking in the small garage that adjoined the east wing, and climbing out of her car. I won't let Father tear my life apart again.

She locked the garage door and went into the house, turning the furnace up to take the chill from the air, and then going straight to the phone. A quick call first to Patrick's school, to alert him to get off the bus at his own house rather than Megan's, and then a call to Megan.

"You're back!" Megan exclaimed. "How was the driving, and was it fun at the school?"

"It was certainly interesting."

"Oh? You'll have to tell me all about it. And your father, how did that go?"

"That was interesting, too," Liane said, realizing she could not possibly describe the events of the past twenty-four hours on the telephone. How melodramatic they would sound! Tycoon Claims Grandson as Heir, Mother Flees into Storm. No, the story would have to wait. "I'll tell you everything that happened the next time we get together, Megan. Thanks so much for keeping Patrick for me—I called the school, and he'll get off the bus here."

"It was a very humbling evening—having wiped me off the board at checkers, he then proceeded to bankrupt Fitz and me at poker. He'll go far, that boy."

"Mars is the present plan. He's saving all my tin cans to build a rocket."

"There's an awful lot you're not saying," Megan remarked. "You wouldn't just whet my appetite?"

"Not right now. I promise I'll give you every grimy detail when I see you."

"I'll hold you to it." Sounding quite violent, red-haired Megan added, "You don't have to do what your father says just because he's got lots of money."

She might not be given the choice. "I know," Liane said.

"Don't you forget it, then," Megan ordered. "Tomorrow's our day in Charlottetown ... want anything?"

"Fitz is getting me the lumber for the bottom three steps in the basement—the wood was rotten, so they had to be taken out, remember? But I don't think I need anything else, thanks. I'd better go, Megan; I have to take something out of the freezer for supper ... talk to you soon."

She put a pan of homemade lasagne out on the counter to thaw, then took her keys and went through the connecting door into the main house, with its luxurious carpets and eighteenth-century oil paintings. Letting herself into the conservatory, she inhaled the familiar damp warmth, scented with orchids and freesias, a miniature haven of tropical color against the backdrop of snow-blanketed woods. She felt very much at home in this room, for she loved caring for all the plants, nurturing them to bloom in the long months of winter. She felt at home; and she felt totally safe. Even now, with the threat of Jake and Chester in the background, she still felt safe.

Shying away from the thought that Jake, for money, had done his best to despoil this safety, Liane noticed a number of small tasks that needed attention. She set to work, and by the time she left the conservatory an hour later she had decided that tomorrow evening she would lay the whole story in front of Megan and Fitz and ask their advice. Fitz, who made rather ugly pots that the tourists seemed to love, concealed a strong streak of practicality under a somewhat Bohemian exterior. Fitz would know what to do.

Fitz would protect her from Jake.

CHAPTER FOUR

Two hours later the yellow school bus stopped by the road and Patrick got out. Liane watched him race down the driveway, his jacket unzipped, his boots unlaced, and felt her heart contract with a long-familiar blend of love and vulnerability. If the lush gardens here at "Riversedge" had helped heal the arid desert of her own childhood, Patrick had preserved her from more adult resentments. For Patrick's father had laughed in her face when she had assumed he would marry her, and her own father had demanded an abortion for the sake of something he called the family honor. Liane had fled from both of them, and, when the red-faced, squalling bundle who was her son had first been placed in her arms, had found out why.

Patrick burst in the door, shucked off his boots on the mat, and cried, "Kim and Clancy are going tobogganning on Mason's Hill—can I go?"

Under his thatch of auburn hair, a legacy from his father, gray eyes that were totally his own looked up at her. She bent to hug him, sensing that today he would be safe from Chester and Jake, wondering how in the future she would deal with situations like this. "I wish you'd tie your boots, Patrick," she said. "I'm always scared you'll trip on the laces."

"Takes too long to take them off if they're done up. Can I, Mom?"

"Yes, you may. Want a glass of milk before you go? How was school today?"

"I got a hundred in maths."

"And English?" Liane asked, head to one side.

"Fifty-seven. It was a stupid test."

"If you're going to be an astronaut you have to be able to write reports. After supper we'll go over the test together. Change into your ski suit, and there are dry mitts on the radiator."

Ten minutes later Patrick was hauling the long wooden toboggan up the hill, waving at his two friends on the road. Liane smoothed out the despised English test, which was a thicket of red marks, and went into the kitchen to make a salad. As the shadows lengthened on the snow and a medley of old Broadway tunes came over the radio, she felt her nerves settle more deeply into the comfort and peace of her home. Jake and Chester would not find her here. She and Patrick were safe.

She carried this conviction through the evening, and because it was so strong she did not tell Patrick about his grandfather's demands; she woke up after a good night's sleep with the same sense of safety. After waving goodbye to Patrick, as he trudged up the hill for the bus, she changed from her housecoat into her oldest jeans and a T-shirt that had shrunk and was consequently no longer wearable in public, and tied her hair in a knot on top of her head. It was time to start some seedlings in the workroom, and when better to do it than this cold, overcast February day?

The workroom was in the opposite wing to her own, a spacious room with a cement floor, banks of fluorescent lighting, and wide windows that overlooked the trees and the distant river, now heaped with ice. Liane turned the radio on to catch the latest news, and began opening the boxes of supplies she had ordered a month ago, piling the green plastic trays on the table and sorting through the packets of seeds, humming as she worked. She grew all the annuals from seed, and a good many of the perennials; it was work she enjoyed, for the tiny green seedlings thrusting up toward the light always inspired in her a kind of tenderness for the forcefulness and fragility of life.

She was almost ready to break for coffee when a movement through the window caught her eye. She glanced up, a big bag of potting soil in her arms. A man was standing outside in the snow, looking in at her through the window, a tall man in a leather jacket. He had black hair and eyes that looked black against the gray sky.

Jake.

For a moment Liane could neither breathe nor move. Imagination, she thought wildly. It's my imagination. But when she blinked he was still there, still staring in at her. A man of darkness against the snow.

Jake. Come to get Patrick. In the one place she had thought she was safe.

With a terror-stricken whimper Liane dropped the bag of soil. It burst, scattering peat moss and vermiculite all over her shoes. Then Jake gesticulated, pointing to the front of the house.

He had rung the doorbell, she thought numbly. He, on the most clandestine of errands, had rung her door as if he were an ordinary visitor on ordinary business. Swallowing a spurt of hysterical laughter, she knew she could not bear to have him staring at her a moment longer. Pivoting, she ran through the door, slamming and locking it behind her, leaning against it as she fought to slow the pounding of her heart.

She had no idea what to do next. The safety she had cocooned herself in for the last twenty-four hours had been an illusion, a dangerous falsity. For the fox had found its prey.

How, she could not imagine. How did not really matter, she thought, drawing a ragged breath. What mattered was what she did next.

No point in phoning Megan or Fitz; they'd gone into the city and wouldn't be back until their two children got home from school. Percy, willing though he might be, was too far away. The police?

She thought of the explanations this would entail, and her spirit quailed. But one thing she could do—must do—was phone the school and make sure Patrick got off the bus at Megan's.

A concrete plan, no matter how small, enabled her to push herself away from the door, to leave her mud-stained shoes on the mat, and to scurry through the Forsters' hallways to the door that led to her wing. She picked up the telephone, spoke in a normal voice to the secretary, and left her message. She then replaced the receiver.

The doorbell chimed.

Her heart gave an exaggerated leap. She crossed the hall to the door, and through the mail slot shouted, "Go away, Jake! Or I'll phone the police."

"I'm not going anywhere until you and I have a talk. So you might as well let me in."

She remembered that tone of voice all too well. She said viciously, "Go back to my father and tell him I don't want anything to do with him, now or ever. Patrick is *my* son. Not——"

"I am not working for your father! Chester is, but I'm not. Let me in—or I'll break in."

"You and Chester are both in his pay!" she cried. "I don't know which of you I despise more. Because I will not let Father get his hands on Patrick, do you hear?"

"You've got it all wrong," Jake said tightly. "I'm not here to take Patrick from you, and I've never met your father——"

"Oh, sure, Jake. You've got the wrong woman—I don't believe in fairy stories any more."

There was a charged silence. Then Jake said, "I'm going to count to ten, Liane. If you haven't opened the door by then, I'm coming in anyway."

The door was oak, with a dead bolt. Like a mouse pinioned by the yellow gaze of a cat, Liane stood very still, and part of her brain was screaming at her to call the police and the other part told her he could not possibly mean what he said. Then she heard a series of small scraping sounds from the other side of the door, and to her horror the doorknob began to turn.

She whirled and saw straight ahead of her the entrance to the basement. There was a door to the back garden in the rear wall of the basement. If she could only get outside she might have a chance to escape, for she knew the terrain like the back of her hand—every tree, every shrub, every hummock in the ground.

The front door swung open. With a choked cry Liane pitched herself down the stairs into the darkness of the cellar, and it was only when she was halfway down that she remembered with a surge of hope that the bottom three steps were missing; after the wood had rotted, Fitz had removed them altogether, claiming they were no longer safe. She knew the steps were missing. Jake did not.

She jumped to the ground, kicked a loose board across the path and ran for the back door, and, with the acute hearing of extreme fear, heard Jake plunge down the steps behind her. As she seized the door handle, Jake suddenly grunted in mingled surprise and alarm, his feet scuffling for a purchase. The loose board banged against the stairwell. Then he gave a bitten-off cry, and through the gloom she saw him fall sideways, saw his frantic clutch at thin air, heard the horrible thud as his head struck the upright beam supporting the ceiling. His body slid to the floor.

In the ominous silence the harsh sound of her own breathing smote her ears. Although she had felt terror when she had taken the stairs two by two, it was nothing like the terror she felt now. She had killed him, she thought, staring fixedly at the dark outline of Jake's body crumpled against the post. She, Liane Daley, who had never committed a violent act in her life, was responsible for a man's death.

Dragging her feet, she approached him, and it never occurred to her that he might be faking. Kneeling on the concrete floor, she took his flaccid wrist in her fingers and felt for the pulse.

It was beating. Strong and sure beneath her fingertips, she felt the pulse of Jake's blood in his veins.

With an incoherent sob Liane scrambled to her feet. She had to call the police now; this had gone too far for her to deal with alone.

The officer on the phone sounded very calm, as though women called up every day to report an unconscious man on their basement floor. He assured her that a patrol car and an ambulance would be there within ten minutes, and hung up. She switched on the basement light and slowly went back down the stairs.

Jake had not moved. She knelt beside him again, her eyes traveling over his face as though she could thereby understand him, and the only conclusion she could reach was that he did not look like a man who would kidnap a child for money. Even with the dark eyes closed, there was the imprint of intelligence and will on Jake's features: the mouth was uncompromising, the profile proud.

She brushed a lock of hair back from his forehead, and saw the wet darkness of blood from his scalp. His hair was soft, and very clean; to touch it filled her with a confusing mixture of panic and, unquestionably, desire.

She had not felt desire since Patrick had been conceived. She had not allowed herself to feel it.

Of their own volition her hands pushed aside the heavy folds of his leather jacket, finding the pulse at the base of his throat, bared by his open-necked shirt. This pulse, too, throbbed against his skin, vital and alive.

Liane sat back on her heels, wishing he would stir, wishing the police would arrive, anything to deliver her from the grip of emotions she thought she had subdued forever. And what a crazy twist of fate that a man she loathed, a man who had, moreover, shown every sign of disliking her, should be the one to arouse these emotions.

Upstairs the bell rang. She clambered up the stairs and went to open the door. A blue and white police car was parked outside and an ambulance was following it down the hill. Two young men in regulation uniform were standing on her step.

She ushered them in, introduced herself, and said baldly, "He's downstairs—the bottom steps are missing, and he fell. He broke in the front door."

One of the officers looked at the lock, then said briefly, "Professional job. Let's take a look."

"You go ahead, I'll take the medics in."

So once more Liane went down to the basement, where Jake was still lying exactly where she had left him. Swiftly the policeman went through Jake's pockets, extracting a leather wallet, and flipping through the assortment of cards it contained. Then, with a small whistle of consternation, his hands stilled. "Well, ma'am," he said, "you caught yourself a good one."

"Wh-what do you mean?" she faltered. Was Jake a known criminal? Did he have a record? Not Jake, she thought painfully. Please, not Jake.

"This guy's a top-ranking officer in the international force."

Liane's jaw dropped. "You mean he's a *policeman*?"

"He sure is." The young man looked at her through narrowed eyes. "Just why was he breaking into your house?"

"To kidnap my son," she said faintly, and to her infinite relief saw a paramedic come down the stairs with a collapsible stretcher. If Jake was a policeman, he couldn't be in her father's pay...could he?

She rubbed at her forehead, wondering if any minute she would wake up under the blue duvet in her own bed and find this had all been a bizarre nightmare. As the medic checked Jake over, she asked even more faintly, "How is he?"

"Concussion—shouldn't be anything serious," the medic replied with a cheerfulness that grated on Liane's nerves. "An X-ray'll be in order, though. Do you want to come with us in the ambulance, miss?"

"I'll bring her," the policeman said. "Once she's answered a few questions."

With professional speed the two medics strapped Jake's body to the stretcher. Then, with the help of one of the policemen, the stretcher was carried up the stairs and out of the door, a process during which Liane discovered how strongly she did want to go with Jake in the ambulance. In the kitchen she patiently went over the events of the last couple of days, rather heartened by the flicker of amusement in the officer's eyes as she described the intervention of the manure spreader. She had no idea whether he believed a word she had said; she was not sure she would, were she him. When she had finished, he closed his notebook, and said stolidly, "We'll check Mr. Brande's credentials and get back to you, Miss Daley. Shall I drive you to the hospital?"

"Please," answered Liane, and grabbed her pink jacket from the cupboard.

At the hospital she was kept waiting until Jake was settled in a room. "He's only in for observation," the daunting, gray-haired nurse said. "But you mustn't stay too long."

Liane thought there was a distinct possibility that Jake, if conscious, would instantly show her the door. "I won't," she promised, and crept into the room.

Jake was lying flat on the bed, his face almost as pale as the sheets, his eyes closed. She tiptoed closer, wondering if he had been drugged, knowing that no matter what he had done she was deeply grateful that he was alive. There was a neat white patch over the wound on his head; she reached out a hand to brush his hair back from his face, and knew that what she really wanted to do was cradle his head to her breast and hold him there.

For a moment her hand was arrested in midair. She hated him. She feared him. She despised him. Yet she wanted to hold him in her arms and comfort him...

As if she were under a spell, watching another woman altogether, she followed the drift of her fingers as they very gently touched his cheek and moved toward his hair.

Jake's eyes flew open, staring straight into her eyes that were so close to his and so bemused. In a blur of movement he circled her wrist with fingers as cold as a handcuff. "What the devil do you think you're doing?"

"I—I don't know," Liane stammered, and knew her words for the literal truth.

"Trying to finish me off? Since the clever little trick with the missing steps didn't work?"

"Of course not! I was terrified that I'd killed you."

"Yeah?" With his other hand he flicked at the loose tendrils of blond hair curving around her cheeks. "I rue the day I ever associated the word dumb with you... you're about as dumb as a rattlesnake. And just as deadly."

Liane had been quite prepared to apologize for what she had done. But she was not prepared to let him walk all over her. "Try looking at it my way, Jake Brande," she fumed. "A man twice my size who's been following me for two days jimmies the lock on my front door, and breaks into my house—you think I should have smiled at you sweetly and made you a nice cup of tea and then handed over my son?" She glowered at him, her mouth a mutinous line. "Not likely."

"I do not want your son!" Jake roared. "Will you get that through your thick head?"

"Then what the hell *do* you want?" she yelled back.

In a crackle of starched skirts the nurse marched in the door and impaled Liane with a glare like a gimlet. "I shall have to ask you to leave!" she announced. "The patient must not get overexcited."

Jake directed a smile at the nurse that would have melted a glacier, and said pacifically, "It was all my fault...will you let her stay just a few more minutes if I promise it won't happen again?"

Something approaching a smile creaked across the matron's face. "Very well," she agreed, "five minutes more." She swept out of the room without deigning to look at Liane again.

"Boy," said Liane, "you sure know how to turn on the charm, don't you? Why haven't you ever tried that little gambit on me?"

Jake loosened his hold on her wrist, smoothing the skin with his fingers in a way she tried futilely to ignore, and remarked, "Your cheeks are the same color as your shirt. Is it your son's shirt? It certainly doesn't look as though it was made to fit an adult."

Liane flushed an even brighter pink. "With you bleeding on the concrete floor and looking as though you were dead, and with policemen and ambulances all over the place, it didn't occur to me to change my shirt," she hissed.

Jake's gaze wandered in a leisurely fashion from her face to her breasts, outlined faithfully by the clinging pink fabric. "I'm very glad it didn't."

She yanked her wrist free, hugged her jacket around her body, and said the first thing that came into her mind. "Are you really a policeman?" she demanded. "'A top-ranking officer in the international force,' quote, unquote?"

"Yeah...I've been overseas for the last four years. Up in Ottawa they haven't figured out what they're going to do with me yet—that's why I've got time off."

Her father had money and power; but not even her father could have subverted the entire police force. Liane said flatly, "So you're not in my father's pay?"

"No. Chester is, though. As I believe I might have mentioned in our discussion through the mail slot."

"I thought both of you were," Liane admitted, frowning at him, and by no means ready to forgive him yet. "Hence the manure spreader."

"Ah, yes, my introduction to farming at its most elemental level...I will admit that the manure spreader was one of the reasons I turned up on your doorstep this morning." Very gingerly Jake patted the bandage in his hair. "I deserve to be fired for falling—literally— for your little trick with the basement stairs, though."

Subduing an emotion that was unquestionably guilt, Liane asked coldly, "So what were the other reasons you broke into my house, Jake?"

"Haven't you guessed?" In another of those lightning-swift moves, he seized her by the elbows, pulled her off balance so that she fell across his chest, and kissed her full on the mouth.

Although Liane was twenty-seven years old and the mother of a son, she was not overly experienced in the art of lovemaking; however, she knew enough to recognize when a kiss began in anger and ended in something else altogether. For the first few moments, moments when she was frozen with surprise, Jake's lips were hard and unyielding, fueled by an emotion as far from tenderness as it could be. But, as she collected her wits and tried to pull away from him, he murmured something deep in his throat, his hands kneading her flesh through her jacket, his kiss gentling seemingly in spite of himself, seeking rather than demanding.

His demands she could have repulsed. His gentleness, a gentleness that seemed entirely out of character, disarmed her. She relaxed. And as she did so she felt desire uncurl within her, licking like flame through her limbs, softening her lips, blanking out everything but the insistence of the present.

"Really!" cried the nurse. "This is quite outrageous!"

Jake raised his head and let go of Liane, who scrambled to her feet beside the bed with less than her usual grace. If her cheeks had been pink earlier, she thought, they must be as red as geraniums now. Quelling an absurd urge to burst out laughing, she said meekly, "I'm truly sorry, he was only kissing me goodbye. Because we won't be seeing each other again."

"Humph," said the nurse. "Mr. Brande has suffered a concussion. *That* is my concern, and my only concern." With a militant gleam in her eye she advanced on Jake and took his pulse. "As I suspected," she said triumphantly, "much too fast. No more visitors today, Mr. Brande." As he opened his mouth to protest, she neatly popped a thermometer in it.

Liane, who had not had as much fun in many months, said limpidly, "Goodbye, Jake; it's been most instructive knowing you. Next time, may I suggest you look before you leap?"

She winked at him, slipped out of the door, and drove home.

CHAPTER FIVE

DESPITE having so sanguinely said goodbye to Jake, Liane was almost sure she had not seen the last of him. In fact, she realized, as she stepped inside, she would be very upset if she thought she would never see him again. And explain that, Liane, she said to herself.

Ahead of her was the door, now closed, to the basement. She gazed at it, lost in thought. He made her feel fully alive, was that it? For, whatever the reason, when she was with him all her emotions were keyed to their highest pitch, be they anger, fear, or—and this was the most difficult one for her to accept—desire.

In the year of Patrick's conception and birth Liane had been so at the mercy of a whirlpool of emotions that afterward she had deliberately set out to make a life for herself where she was protected from such turmoil. Her emotions toward Patrick, of course, she felt to the fullest, and she had been close friends with both Megan and Fitz—she was not afraid of that kind of intimacy. But she dated only rarely, she had had nothing that could be construed even remotely as an affair, and after two or three rebuffs right after Patrick was born she had learned to stay away from her father.

Jake, whom she now knew she had met by chance rather than from any design of her father's, could change all that. He had been rude to her, he had pursued her across three provinces, and he had scared her out of her wits; yet when he had kissed her he had broken through all her defenses. She had not put up even a token struggle.

She hung up her coat and wandered into the kitchen, where through the window the snow and the sky were the same leaden gray. The changes were in her, thought Liane, and felt a frisson of fear course along her spine.

She began to make a meat loaf together with baked potatoes, and the simple task calmed her. She would not see Jake today—the nurse would see to that. And after supper she would ask Megan and Fitz for advice. It wouldn't matter if Patrick was late getting to bed, because it was Friday.

So at six-thirty that evening she was being ushered in the door at Megan's, the two dogs barking at her heels. Both Megan and Fitz were a little larger than life, for Megan was statuesque and full-breasted with a mop of tangled red curls, while Fitz boasted a beard of Old Testament proportions and a booming voice worthy of any prophet. As always, the pots he made for the tourists were scattered throughout the house; only a few people, Liane among them, knew of the very different pieces he kept tucked away in his storeroom, and of the lack of confidence that kept him from displaying them publicly. According to Megan, he was near a breakthrough. Liane, who liked him very much, hoped Megan was right.

Clancy and Kim had already taken Patrick down to the games room to play computer games. Bouncer, a large and endearingly clumsy mongrel, flopped down near the stove, while Trojan the dachshund headed single-mindedly for the food dish. The three adults settled in the untidy, comfortable living room with its wood-stove and thick shag carpet. Fitz had made mulled wine; curving her hands around the warm glass, Liane began to describe the events of the last three days, leaving out nothing but Jake's two kisses.

She could not possibly have complained about her audience, because her two friends were plainly enraptured by her story. When she finished, Megan breathed, "How romantic..."

"Hard to see a manure spreader as romantic," Fitz commented. "Did he make a pass at you, Liane?"

She should have remembered that Fitz was not noted for his tact. She took a gulp of wine, and said primly, "He's scarcely had the opportunity."

"Doesn't sound to me like the kind of guy who'd let that stop him. You figure he's going to turn up on your doorstep tomorrow?"

"Maybe."

"If your father's halfway serious, you'd better let him in. Your father's big problem is that too many people are afraid of him—you included."

"I'm right to be afraid of him, Fitz," she retorted. "I know him better than you do."

Fitz was unabashed. "You're twenty-seven now, not nineteen. Time you took him on." He tugged at his beard, his amber eyes laughing at her. "Hire this Jake as a bodyguard. That'll give him lots of opportunities."

"You're not being very helpful," Liane said crossly.

"Okay, okay—get a pencil and paper, Megan, and let's see what we can do here."

When Liane left two hours later she was carrying a neatly written and very helpful list of suggestions. The one to which Fitz had given priority was that she should tell Patrick everything that had happened. Tomorrow, she thought. Tomorrow's Saturday, I'll tell him then.

She turned off the road down the long slope of the driveway to the Forsters' house. In front of the house, parked with no attempt at concealment, was a cherry red wagon.

The glare of her headlights illuminated the man sitting behind the wheel. It was, of course, Jake.

As strong as it was unexpected, Liane felt an uprush of an emotion she could only call joy. He had come back.

He had not accepted her goodbye as final at all. She said to Patrick with careful truth, "That's a man I met when I stayed at the school; his name is Jake, and he's a policeman. Let's go and see what he wants."

She knew one thing he wanted; keeping her mind firmly away from that, she walked across to the wagon. Jake opened the door and climbed out. "I've been waiting for over an hour," he complained.

Liane had left three outdoor lights on, so it was not difficult to see that he was still frighteningly pale. Nor did she think his tiny stagger when his feet hit the ground was in any way assumed. "You'd better come in," she said formally. "This is my son, Patrick."

Patrick held out his hand, eyeing the white patch on Jake's forehead. "What happened to your head?"

"I fell down some stairs," Jake replied, and shook Patrick's hand as briefly as good manners would allow.

"We've got three stairs that are being fixed," Patrick said, not seeming to notice the brevity of Jake's handshake, and favoring him with an angelic, gap-toothed grin. "You'd better watch out."

"I had indeed," agreed Jake, directing an enigmatic glance at Patrick's mother.

Liane, who had noticed the brevity of the handshake, returned look for look, and said calmly, "I'm sorry you had to wait. But then I didn't know you were coming, did I?"

"You might have guessed that after six hours of head nurse I was in serious danger of a relapse."

In spite of herself her lips quirked. She turned to unlock the front door, switched on the lights, and said to Patrick, "Upstairs and clean your teeth, hon; I'll be up in a minute to say good-night."

For a moment Patrick held his ground, staring up at the tall man standing inside the door. "Did you help my mom when she got stuck in the snow?" he asked. "'Cause you're a policeman?"

For a moment Jake looked nonplussed. Liane said quickly, "Yes, he did. Off you go, Patrick."

"You can come up to my room with her and see my rocket models," Patrick offered, "if you want."

Liane knew this was an invitation not extended to many adults. She held her breath, and heard Jake say, after the smallest of hesitations, "Thank you, I'd like that."

Jake did not want to go up to Patrick's room—she knew that intuitively; yet equally he had not wanted to hurt a small boy's feelings. Suddenly liking him very much, she gave him her most generous smile.

Patrick had taken the stairs to the loft two by two. Jake said roughly, "I've spent a great deal of my career assessing people, with my life often depending on how accurate I was. But you, Liane—I don't have a clue what you're all about. All my training and experience fly out the window when I'm within fifty feet of you."

He did not look friendly. Liane's smile faded. She indicated the door into the living room and said, "You'd better sit down before you fall down—as a policeman, you should have known better than to drive in your condition."

He walked ahead of her into the room, saying impatiently, "I'm fine."

"Sit," Liane ordered.

As Jake sank rather abruptly into the nearest chair, she further hardened her heart. "I assume you're booked into a motel?"

"No." With a ghost of a smile he said, "I'm here to protect you."

How pleased Fitz would be with this turn of events, Liane thought sardonically. "So you're planning to move

in? Were you thinking of asking permission, or isn't that
on your agenda?"

He said flatly, "I know fear when I see it—and you're
a frightened woman. I don't like what you're doing to
your father, but I didn't like Chester very much, either.
So you're stuck with me for now, until I figure out what's
going on."

She clenched her fists. "What do you mean, what *I'm*
doing to my——?"

Patrick's voice wafted down from the loft, "Mom,
I'm ready."

"I haven't told Patrick anything about Chester or my
father yet," Liane announced, glaring at Jake. "I don't
want you saying anything."

Jake got to his feet, standing only six inches from her.
"I'm sure you don't," he replied with equal anger.

She had no idea what he meant. Tossing her head,
she marched out of the room and up the stairs, Jake
following her, and it took an actual physical effort for
her to say pleasantly, at the top of the stairs, "The
Forsters very kindly remodelled the attic into a room for
Patrick . . . it's nice, isn't it?"

"The Forsters?"

"The people who own the house."

"*You* don't?"

Liane gave him an astounded look. "Are you kidding?
I'm lucky to be able to afford the rent."

"The Forsters live in Florida all winter," Patrick explained. "Mom's their gardener. My models are over
here."

He was wearing an old tracksuit emblazoned with the
insignia of the Edmonton Oilers, and his hair was
standing up in spikes all over his head. Liane glanced
over at Jake, who was still standing in the doorway, and
felt his reluctance to enter as palpably as if it had been
her own. She had never felt so at loss with anyone before,

so lacking in understanding; she said lightly, "Watch your head, Jake; this room wasn't built for men over six feet."

He crossed the room and bent to the models. Liane did a little perfunctory tidying, listening to the two voices, Patrick's so familiar and well-loved, Jake's deeper one making all the right responses, yet somehow dead. She threw five dirty socks in the hamper, wondering where the sixth one was and why mittens and socks never got lost in pairs. Then she straightened, gazing aimlessly out of the window into the darkness that lay over the river. Patrick loved his room. If Jake's presence enabled her to keep both Chester and her father at bay so that she and Patrick could stay here, then Jake must stay. For as long as necessary. Or for as long as he was willing.

Jake had said good-night. Liane crossed the room, hugged Patrick close, and whispered the ritual words. "Sleep well. I love you."

"Love you too, Mom. G'night."

She left the night-light on, and followed Jake down the stairs and into the living room. As he turned to face her, she went on the attack. "I have one question—how did you find out where I live?"

"Your licence plate—I pulled rank and got access to the files."

"Oh. Can Chester do that?"

"No. But he'll find you sooner or later; it's almost impossible in a place as small as this for you to stay hidden."

She looked straight at him. "I do need your help, Jake. My father wants Patrick, and he won't be scrupulous about his methods... Can I hire you, even if it's only for a few days, to keep an eye on Patrick?"

There was not a trace of expression on Jake's face. "I've got a month's leave—you don't have to pay me."

"I'd prefer to. This is a business deal."

"For you, maybe," he said. "Yes, I'll stay—although not necessarily for the reasons you might think."

"I don't want to know what your reasons are!"

His eyes narrowed as he stepped closer. "Oh, don't you?" he grated. Then he grabbed her by the shoulders and bent his head to kiss her.

Liane could have avoided him or pushed him away, for he did not look as though he wanted to kiss her. Rather, he looked like a man driven to do so, and strongly resenting his own compulsions. Instead she stood still, achingly aware of the warmth and weight of his hands, of the fierce demand of his lips, of her own wild and wayward response, so undeniable and so immediate. She could not hide it; she did not want to. She swayed toward him, her body molding itself to his, and opened willingly to the first dart of his tongue.

Time vanished. Thought vanished. She was drowning in sweetness, in the throb of her blood and the hot, red insistence of desire, too long subdued. Jake's hands were roaming the curve of her spine, straining her to him, even as her fingers traced the breadth of his shoulders and then buried themselves in his hair. She had forgotten about the wound in his scalp. Inadvertently she touched the dressing, and felt the flinch of pain travel the length of his body.

She pulled free, saying in distress, "Jake, I'm sorry..."

He was breathing hard, his eyes dark shadowed and full of turmoil. He asked harshly, "Are you always that willing?"

Feeling as though he had slapped her, Liane said, "I was that willing once before. Patrick is the result." And then, because she was essentially a truthful woman, she added with a puzzled frown, "Although in all honesty I don't remember ever wanting Noel as much as I just wanted you."

For a moment Jake looked visibly disconcerted. Then, almost as though another man had taken over, he sneered, "You expect me to believe that?"

"I'd like you to," she said evenly. "Because it happens to be true."

He ran a finger down the side of her face, and she knew in her bones that he did not mean it as a caress. "So Noel is Patrick's father."

"That's right."

"Why didn't you marry him? Wasn't he rich like your father?"

She struck his hand away, suddenly furious. "I don't have to take this, Jake! If you like so little of me, why do you keep on kissing me as though I'm the last woman on earth, and why the *hell* did you bother tracking me down all the way from the Wentworth Valley to here?"

"If I knew the answer to that question, I probably wouldn't be here!"

He looked as angry with himself as with her. Ignoring this, Liane swept on, "Then let me make something clear—I'm not looking for a father for Patrick—I like my life just the way it is, and if you think you're going to have a cozy little affair with me in return for watching over Patrick you're quite wrong! That's not in the cards. I don't have affairs—the cost's too high. So if that's why you're here, now's your chance to leave."

She had run out of words and breath at the same time. Fitz would not have approved of her last speech, she thought, trying to calm the racing of her blood in her veins, and wondering what she would do if Jake walked out of the door. Call him back? Slam it behind him? Burst into tears?

"Why didn't you marry Noel, Liane?"

She was too upset for anything but the truth. "Because he laughed in my face when I suggested it. A good enough reason, wouldn't you say?"

For several long seconds Jake was silent. Then he said, raising one brow, "Did he now? Perhaps he was afraid of your temper. How often does Patrick see him?"

"Noel made it very clear he did not want at any time to see the baby he was fifty per cent responsible for and that I was foolish enough to want to keep. I got in touch with him when Patrick was born, but he was too busy getting ready to move to Vancouver to visit either one of us."

Her blue eyes were bleak. Patrick's birth had taught her about vulnerability, and she had been deeply hurt that the man who had fathered her son had not even wanted to see him. Then she shrugged her shoulders. "It's over now, done with. Are you staying or leaving?"

"Oh, I'm staying. You're more of a mystery than nine-tenths of the cases I've worked on."

Liane's first emotion was relief that she would not have to face Chester alone, her second, fear that she was letting a man as powerful and inimical as Jake within her four walls. Her third, as she looked up at his drawn white face, was compassion. "I don't have a spare bedroom," she said. "But the couch here is a sofa bed; I'll make it up for you, and get you some towels . . . do you have a suitcase?"

"In the wagon."

She started taking the cushions off the couch. "I'll get it for you—and don't argue."

"You're a very strong-willed woman."

She flashed him a wicked grin. "Whereas you, I would suspect, are quite unaccustomed to taking orders from anyone. Least of all a female."

As he suddenly smiled back, a smile that transformed his face, Liane dropped a cushion. "Your suspicions are entirely correct," he said.

She scurried from the room to find sheets and towels. When she came back, Jake had disappeared into the bathroom. She made up the bed, drew the curtains, and put a glass of water on the table by the bed. Then she went outside to get his case.

The clouds had cleared a little, so that patches of stars were intermingled with larger patches of blackness; it was very quiet. Her footsteps crunching on the ice, she pulled his case from the floor of the wagon, and saw that the tattered flight tickets still attached to the handle were from Hong Kong, Bangkok, and Vancouver. It seemed very strange that this tall, dark-haired man who was such an enigma to her should have ended up on the shores of a river thousands of miles from any of those places. Even stranger that he would be sleeping only a few feet away from her.

She eased the tension from her shoulders, not liking the direction her thoughts were taking her, and shut the door of the wagon. Then she lugged the case, which was very heavy, into the house and across the hall. Jake was still in the bathroom. After heaving the case onto the old pine blanket box by the wall, she turned to leave the living room.

Jake was blocking the doorway; she had not heard even a whisper of his steps. She said disagreeably, "I wish you wouldn't sneak up on me like that."

"You'd better get used to it—one of the hazards of living with a policeman."

His smile had not reached his eyes. He stayed where he was, leaning against the doorframe as he let his gaze wander around the room, with its unpretentious furniture and its inexpensive framed prints. "This must be a far cry from your father's living room," he said, a wealth of innuendo in his voice.

"Thank goodness," retorted Liane, her chin tilting defiantly.

She knew it was not the answer he had been looking for. He snapped, "You don't have to play games with me, Liane. I'm in your pay—it's far better that you be honest."

"Jake," she said forcefully, "I'm tired, and you look as though the only thing keeping you upright is the door post. I have a very busy day tomorrow, but I promise that once Patrick is in bed you and I will sit down in here and you can unburden your soul of the multifarious suspicions you're harboring toward me. But we will not do that tonight, thank you very much!"

"When you get angry, your vocabulary goes haywire," he remarked. "Tomorrow night—it's a date."

"It is not a date," Liane retorted, her cheeks still flushed, "it's a business arrangement."

Jake straightened with the lazy grace that she already recognized as characteristic of him. "Besides being a mystery, you're also extremely argumentative. Out, Liane. Unless you want me, despite my present decrepitude, to take you to bed."

Hovering at the back of her mind had been just that possibility, she realized, appalled that she could even consider it. Schooling her face to what she hoped was a noncommittal smile, she said, "Not what the nurse would recommend after a concussion... good night, Jake."

"I don't think the nurse would recommend it at any time," was the dry response. "Detrimental to the blood pressure and bad for the heart. Not to mention the morals."

Liane choked back a laugh and left the room, closing the door behind her. She had invited far more than a bodyguard for Patrick into her house, she thought, crossing the hall to her own room. But she was not nineteen any more; she was a mature woman who was quite capable of keeping Jake Brande in his place. In his own room. In his own bed.

And she in hers.

CHAPTER SIX

WHEN Liane got up about nine the next morning and went to the bathroom for a leisurely shower, the scent of Jake's after-shave was the first impression to penetrate her sleep-fogged brain. So when she went into the kitchen half an hour later, she was not surprised to find him sitting by the window with his feet propped up, reading the paper.

He looked very much at home. Too much so.

Patrick was at the table, surrounded by a litter of cornflake crumbs, reading the comics. With his mouth full he mumbled, "Hi, Mom. Garfield's neat; you gotta read it."

Jake looked up. Liane was wearing tailored trousers with a mohair sweater she had knitted last winter, in varying shades of blue. She had pulled her hair on top of her head in a loose knot, and her face was innocent of makeup. "Morning," he said. "Coffee's made." And he went back to the paper.

Liane, who preferred to be ignored first thing in the morning, found herself resenting both Patrick and Jake for ignoring her now. Don't be such a grump, she chided herself, and buried her nose in her coffee mug. The coffee was delicious. A man of many talents, she thought uncharitably, and grabbed the middle section of the newspaper.

Her edginess seemed to accumulate as the day went by, as the three of them bought groceries, got Patrick's hockey skates sharpened, and did several errands in town. She could not blame it on Jake, for he was polite

without being intrusive, and she could not have faulted
the inconspicuous way he kept an eye on her son. Neither
was it Patrick's fault; Patrick had an easygoing dispo-
sition that every morning she envied. The fault was hers,
she thought unhappily, starting to put the groceries away
as Patrick raced into the living room to watch his favorite television program, and wishing Jake could be
equally interested in the exploits of the starship
Enterprise.

Jake said softly, "Relax, Liane."

She shoved the garbage bags under the sink, and said
with at least partial truth, "I'm not used to having
anyone else around all the time. Except for Patrick."

"If I'm going to be here for a month, you'd better
get used to it."

A month sounded like forever. A life sentence. Aware
with every nerve in her body of him standing only two
feet away from her, hating herself for this awareness,
Liane said desperately, "Do you want broccoli or peas
with roast beef?"

"Broccoli. Shall I peel the potatoes?"

"You're behaving more like a husband than a bodyguard," she cried, and then could have bitten off her
tongue.

"In my day I've been both," Jake answered. "Your
vegetable knife needs sharpening."

Her fingers gripping the broccoli as tightly as if it were
about to run away, she said, "There's a whetstone in the
drawer by the stove. Are you still married?"

"Divorced. Five years ago. Have you got some oil?"

She put the broccoli down very carefully, reached into
one of the lower cupboards, and held the can out to
him. "Didn't she like you being a policeman?"

Jake grabbed the oil from her. "Don't pry."

But she had seen the tightening of his jaw, the barricading of his eyes against her. "You brought the subject up... is she the reason you hate women?"

"You're making several very facile assumptions right now," he said tautly. "And I have no intention of starting a fight when Patrick's in the next room."

She had forgotten about Patrick. Jake had been here less than twenty-four hours and already she knew her house was too small for three people when one of the three was a large and highly disturbing male. Wishing she could banish him to the Forsters' part of the house, knowing that was impossible, Liane busied herself with the roast and tried to maintain a dignified silence.

But Jake would not let her. He wanted to know how much broccoli, he couldn't find the saucepans, he then decided to sharpen her carving knife, and before she knew it they were comparing likes and dislikes among everything from vegetables to popular music. It was all so domesticated, Liane concluded later in mixed exasperation and pleasure as Jake carved the roast, a task she always hated. *Was* this how husbands behaved?

Fitz loved cooking, his speciality being curries hot enough to necessitate the consumption of quantities of beer. Liane stared into the green florets of the broccoli, knowing she had often marveled at the laughter, the stormy fights, and the deep companionship of Fitz and Megan's marriage. Marveled, yet never expected that she herself could have such a marriage.

Her mother, to the best of her knowledge, had never raised her voice to her father. But then, her mother had died when Liane was only seven, so what did she know about it?

"The meat's getting cold, Liane."

Liane gaped up at Jake as though she had never seen him before, and blurted, "I think that for a marriage to work the couple has to be able to fight. What do you think?''

For a moment he looked truly amused. "There's one thing about you—I never know what you're going to say next; I was expecting a profundity on the nature of green vegetables, not on marriage. I'm not the one to ask— my wife left me."

As he took the saucepan from her and drained it in the sink, a cloud of steam fogged up the window. "And I bet you've never told anyone how you feel about *that*!" Liane asserted.

"You'd better call Patrick, hadn't you?" Jake suggested pleasantly. "Supper's ready."

Baffled, knowing she would get no more confidences from him, Liane did as he suggested. The meal was delicious. After the dishes were done, they all played cards around the kitchen table, and, because Jake was every bit as quick-witted as she and Patrick, there was a great deal of laughter and bantering. When she glanced up at the clock, Liane exclaimed, "Goodness, it's nine-thirty, Patrick—bedtime!"

"One more hand, Mom—he's ahead of me."

"Just one, then."

Patrick, scowling in concentration, eventually laid down four of a kind, thereby defeating Jake. Jake laughed, reached out to ruffle Patrick's hair, and then suddenly stopped, his hand frozen in midair, his face a rictus of agony. Patrick did not notice, being absorbed in gathering the cards and shuffling them. Liane, who had noticed, found herself instinctively glancing away, for whatever the source of Jake's emotion she was sure it was intensely private.

Jake has a son, she thought, knew her words for the truth, and said matter-of-factly, "Brush your teeth, Patrick; I'll be up in a minute."

Patrick grinned at Jake. "Will you be here tomorrow night? Can we play again?"

Jake had himself fully in control. "I guess so," he said.

It was enough for Patrick, who ran upstairs to get ready for bed. Liane put away the cards. Jake stared out of the window.

Fifteen minutes later, after Liane had said good-night to her son, she and Jake went into the living room. Liane sat down in the wing chair, and Jake on the sofa across from her. The interrogation can begin, thought Liane, who was feeling very nervous, and equally determined not to show it.

Jake took the initiative. "I've decided that if you still want to hire me I'll take whatever salary you think you can afford—that way we'll be on a business footing."

Liane had expected to have to fight for this. Deflated, she named an amount. Jake nodded in agreement. Then he said, "Why don't you tell me your version of events— why were you so frightened at the schoolhouse?"

"I'll tell you the truth," Liane rejoined crisply, and proceeded to do so, beginning with the day nearly three weeks ago when she had read about her brother's death in the paper. "I went to the funeral, of course, even though my brother and I had never been close. My father scarcely seemed to know what was going on; he was in shock, I suppose. I felt sorry for him, so two weeks later—last Wednesday, the day we met—I went to see him again." Scarcely aware of her audience, she grimaced. "Big mistake. He'd had the time to think, and he presented me with an ultimatum. Because of my brother's death he'd lost his heir. He wants Patrick to be his new heir, to live with him in his house, to be groomed to take over the family business...I could move back into the family home, but Patrick would be sent to private school in the winters and to camp every summer."

Unable to sit still, she prowled over to the window and gazed out into the darkness. "I refused. He threatened me with any number of dire consequences. I left. Whereupon, as you know, Chester followed me and I eventually got home."

"What sort of threats?"

"To kidnap Patrick. And then, if I tried to get him back, to take me to court and sue for custody. He would, he said, produce witnesses to say I'd been a drug user, had had casual affairs, was not a fit mother...oh, on and on." Keeping her voice level with an immense effort, she finished, "They're ridiculous accusations. But it's entirely possible he would succeed. Money will make people swear black is white if need be."

Jake said calmly, "I would have thought there would have been many advantages for Patrick, living with his grandfather. The best education money can buy, opportunities to travel..."

She turned to face him. "I happen to disagree."

"Why, Liane?" Jake asked, his eyes as impenetrable as the night beyond the window.

"Because I will not force upon him the kind of upbringing I had!"

"Ah...now we're getting to it. You hate your father, don't you?"

She said with scrupulous accuracy, "I thoroughly dislike some aspects of his behavior. Nor does he love Patrick."

"You've never given him the chance to."

His voice had the bite of steel. Hearing her blood thrum in her ears, Liane asked, "What are you getting at, Jake?"

"Let's try a slightly different version, shall we? From motives of revenge you've kept Patrick from his grandfather ever since he was born. Now, with your brother's death, you're suddenly in an excellent bargaining position. If your father wants to see Patrick he has to go through you; and he's going to have to pay through the nose. *That's* why you were so terrified at the school— you were afraid your father was having you followed and would find out where Patrick lives. Blow your cover. Because if your father can turn up on your doorstep to see Patrick any time he likes, you won't make a cent, will you? So of course you want to keep your son out of sight.''

Jake's voice had not altered in pitch; his eyes were trained on her face. Liane took a deep breath. "You don't really believe that," she stated.

"Your father's a very rich man. And it's pretty obvious you don't have much in the way of worldly goods."

Feeling as though an abyss had just opened in front of her, Liane replied with a steadiness of which, dimly, she was proud, "I have a great deal. I have a son who loves me and whom I love more than anyone else in the world. I have good friends. I have work that I enjoy, and I'm lucky enough to live in a place I find very beautiful... These are the things that matter to me. Not my father's money."

Jake got up and walked over to her, his eyes never leaving her. "How very pure minded of you. Are you saying you've never hankered after even a fraction of your father's fortune?"

"No, I'm not saying that! There have been times when I've been desperate for money. But I won't jump to his tune—not for anything will I do that, and if he said that I would then he's wrong."

"I've never met your father," Jake retorted, "I keep telling you that. Chester is the one who told me the game you're playing."

"At the manure spreader," Liane said slowly, and gave a rather wild giggle. "How very symbolic. And you chose to believe a hired thug instead of me?"

"I believed the version that made sense of the facts."

Her eyes glittering, she struck. "So why did you follow me, if I'm nothing but an unprincipled, manipulative money grabber?"

He seized her by the arm. "In the five years since my wife left you're the only woman I've met who's got under my skin—and make sense of that if you can," he challenged furiously.

"I sure don't understand how you can be attracted to a woman you despise," she retaliated, and then winced as the words replayed themselves mockingly in her ears. She was attracted to Jake. Even now, when he was glaring at her in hatred and frustration, and when he had just finished tearing her character into shreds, she felt the pull of her body to his, the joined throbbing of their blood.

Fighting against it, yet knowing it to be deeper than herself, stronger than rationality, she added shrewishly, "You can't be much of a policeman if you allow your hormones to lead you around the countryside."

He snarled, "Oh, you're not the only reason I'm here. There's another player involved, or have you forgotten him? Patrick. I'm here for Patrick's sake."

"Then why aren't you ushering Patrick's grandfather up the front path?" she cried.

His grip tightened unconsciously. "I'm not a fool, Liane. Murray Hutchins has built a commercial empire for himself, and you don't do that by being a nice guy. I'm prepared to admit your father could be ruthless in the pursuit of something he wants—and that's where I come in. I won't have Patrick being made a pawn between you. Played one against the other like a wild card.

That's why I'm here. To protect Patrick from both of you.''

Her eyes blazing, Liane spat, "You'd be better employed looking after your own son!"

The color drained from Jake's face, and his fingers loosened their hold. "How do you know about my son?" he whispered.

If ever she had seen raw pain in a man's face, Liane saw it now, and she had been the cause of it. "I—I'm sorry," she faltered, "I shouldn't have said that." Her voice gathered strength. "But *my* son isn't your business, Jake—I've looked after him for seven years on my own, and I don't want the help of someone who hates me. If I can hire you, I can also fire you—and that's what I'm doing right now. I want you gone from here tomorrow. You can say goodbye to Patrick in the morning and then leave."

"No."

She shook her arm free. "You'll do as I say! This is *my* home and I'm the one to decide who comes in that door and who stays."

He was fully in command of himself again. "Not in this case, Liane. I'm here and I'm staying."

Beside herself with fury, Liane said incoherently, "I'll *make* you leave!"

"How?" he queried gently. "You can't call the police. Anyway, if you really are afraid that Patrick might be kidnapped, I would have thought you'd be begging me to stay."

Her nails were digging into the palms of her hands; she had never felt such a turmoil of frustration and rage. Because, of course, Jake was right. She *was* afraid that Patrick would be kidnapped. And Jake, for all his one-sided view of her motives, would not allow anyone to take her son against his will.

She bit her lip, trying to still the racing of her heart, striving to calm herself. "Promise me something, then," she said, looking straight up at him. "Swear you won't take Patrick to his grandfather's or get in touch with Chester."

"For a period of one month I swear I won't do either one. Beyond that, I won't swear to anything."

Liane's shoulders sagged. She had won a month's grace. For a month Patrick would be safe. "Thank you," she said quietly.

"Do you know what drives me crazy about you?" he exploded. "It's as though you've got two faces. The one is so goddamned beautiful—the curve of your cheekbone, your skin smooth as the petal of a flower, the blue depths of your eyes—yet you'd cheat an old man out of seeing his only grandson. And how in hell do I reconcile that with the rest of you?"

Liane suddenly wanted to weep, for it had been a long time—too long—since a man had looked on her with the eyes of wonderment and desire; and now it was a man who thought her soul was as tawdry as outwardly he found her beautiful. She said with the courage of desperation, "I can only be myself, Jake. Sometimes I don't think you're seeing me at all—you're seeing other women, stereotyping me. I don't know who they are or what they did to you...but you're judging me as if I were one of them."

For a long moment Jake was silent, his face shadowed and withholding. Then he moved his shoulders restlessly and stepped back from her. "It can't be that simple," he muttered.

Liane stayed where she was, aware that at some level she was as exhausted as if she'd scrubbed down the greenhouse or dug up the perennial bed. Her shoulders ached and her legs were weak. She said, trying to keep her voice from shaking, "I'll see you in the morning.

Patrick has a hockey game at eight at the rink in Centreville, so we'll have to be up early."

Jake shot her a quick glance. "I can take him."

"I always go." Her grin was self-deprecating. "One-woman cheering section."

"Okay. I'll be up."

He gave her a curt nod. She slipped past him, and went to her own room and closed the door. Standing at the window, she stared down at the river, where the faint gleam of a new moon silvered the water. In the last few minutes it had become quite clear to her what she wanted in the next month. She wanted Jake to believe in her. To see her as she really was.

The alarm startled Liane out of a confusing dream in which she and Chester were chasing a polar bear down by the river, and the bear when it turned at bay had the face of her father. She sat bolt upright, jammed her finger on the switch to stop the beeping, and put her feet to the floor, knowing from experience that it was fatal to lie down again. Scarcely awake, she stumbled to the bathroom.

Jake was just coming out of there. Liane blinked, and clutched the semitransparent folds of her nightgown to her chest. "Oh—I'd forgotten about you."

It was obvious that she was speaking the truth, and that seduction was the last thing on her mind. Jake's eyes raked her from head to toe, missing not one detail from her tumbled curls to the pale jut of her hipbone under the thin blue nylon. "I wish I could say the same," he rasped.

An angry Jake at 7:00 a.m. was more than Liane could handle. "Make yourself useful, Jake," she sputtered, "and go put the coffee on. I can't face the rink without at least one cup."

Uncannily he echoed her perceptions of the day before. "You know what's driving me crazy? This is all so domesticated—sharing the bathroom, cooking dinner, playing cards at the kitchen table. But we're not married, are we, Liane?" Very deliberately he ran one finger from her throat to the curve of her collarbone, and, as he did so, his wrist brushed her breast.

She could not have prevented her tiny indrawn breath, for in his touch was all the magic of spring and the heat of summer. But he hated her, she thought frantically. And it was not summer. It was winter. She backed into the bathroom, praying he would not try to stop her. "I won't be long," she muttered, and closed the door in his face.

She squinted at her disheveled hair and sleep-warm lips in the mirror. A month of living with Jake? It would drive her crazy, too. To start with, she must get in the habit of wearing a housecoat. And the first time she went into the city she was going to buy him a different brand of after-shave.

Fifteen minutes later, while Patrick told Jake in exhaustive detail about the exploits of his team, the Hilldale Tigers, Liane sat down to drink a mug of coffee and eat a piece of toast. Jake then warmed up the wagon, scraped the ice from the windshield, and helped Patrick haul the big canvas bag of gear outdoors. Liane said, still not fully awake as Jake held the passenger door open for her, "Life's certainly a lot easier with a man around."

"So anyone would do—just as long as he's male? Thanks a lot."

"Jake, you're as grumpy as I am in the mornings," she observed roundly. "Besides, I never said you were just anyone."

Something flared in Jake's eyes. Hurriedly Liane clambered into her seat, and allowed Patrick to chatter all the way to the rink. The parking lot was already crowded with vehicles and small boys. Patrick disappeared into the dressing room, and Liane led Jake up into the bleaches, where several other parents were already sitting, huddled in blankets against the early morning cold. Quickly she went down the row of names. "Margot and Sean, Danny, Brian, Jean, Bill and Lindy... this is Jake, a friend who's staying for a few days."

"Hi there, Jake," Bill said, moving over a little to make room for him. "Where do you hail from?"

Feeling a little as though she had cast Jake to the lions, Liane chatted to Lindy and listened with one ear to Jake fielding questions with a skill that amused her. The boys came out on the ice and warmed up. Then the game started.

Liane had long ago decided that, if she was going to drag herself out of bed before dawn in the middle of winter, she was going to enjoy the games when she got there. So she yelled and clapped and booed, groaning as Patrick missed a shot on goal, laughing as five boys tumbled one over the other in front of the net. The final score was a tie. She grinned over at Jake. "That was fun, wasn't it?"

She was wearing a bright pink ski suit with white fur mittens, her cheeks as pink as her suit, her eyes sparkling. Bill was stretching his legs, explaining the referee's last call to his wife; Jake said softly, "I'd like to be carrying you off to bed right now."

Liane's heart leaped in her breast. Caught by his eyes, black as night, she was pulled to him as magnets were pulled: by lines of force invisible to the beholder. He was not touching her. He had no need to, she thought wildly, for he was surrounding her, holding her in a way that had nothing to do with either words or touch. His power was immense; she would have gone with him anywhere he asked.

Then Bill leaned over, holding out a gloved hand. "Nice to have met you, Jake," he said bluffly. "See you around. See you, Liane. Our boys did a good job, didn't they? But they sure gotta work on their defense."

The spell was broken. Liane stood up, her eyes downcast, and followed the others to the dressing room. Patrick rehashed the game on the way home; she made a big breakfast of omelets and muffins, and then disappeared to her room to read while Patrick did his homework.

After a late lunch, she and Patrick walked down to the river to watch the ducks circling in the open water where currents kept the ice from forming. As the two of them tramped across the frozen marsh grass, Liane said, knowing she had to do this but hating every minute of it, "Patrick, there's something I need to talk to you about."

"I studied English for a whole half hour," he said.

"It's not that—it's about your grandfather." Choosing her words with care, she explained what had happened on her last visit, and described Chester to him. "So I don't want you talking to any strangers, or getting in anyone's car, okay? And Jake's here to keep an eye on you, too."

Patrick's eyes grew round. "Like a security man when you get to be prime minister? Has he got a gun?"

"I sincerely hope not!"

"I'm going to ask him. Wow, that's neat!"

"But you mustn't tell anyone at school."

His face fell. "Not even Clancy?"

"Not even him. Jake is just a friend who's visiting us for a while."

"Oh... I thought perhaps he was your boyfriend, and that maybe you and him'd get married," Patrick said, slanting a look up at her through lashes as long as her own.

"No, darling," Liane replied, and for once did not correct his grammar.

Golden-eyed ducks, neatly patterned in black and white, were swimming in the channel in the middle of the river. She and Patrick watched them for a while then wandered back to the house. Jake had parked his wagon in the garage, and was fiddling with the engine; Patrick went to join him, and Liane heard him say, "Mom told me you're my bodyguard, like the pope or the president. You got a gun?"

Not waiting to hear the answer, Liane went indoors. Patrick had never before raised the possibility that she might get married, or that he in any way craved the kind of home life that most of his friends took for granted. She felt a surge of anger against her father, that because of him Jake's presence was such a necessity. For Jake, just by being here, would bring change. Of that she was sure.

CHAPTER SEVEN

THAT evening the three of them were invited to Megan's for dinner. Liane had brought a cyclamen from the greenhouse, the plant a mass of showy pink blooms. Holding it out of Bouncer's reach, she gave it to Megan once they were in the door. Megan buried her face in it, laughing at her own enthusiasm. "I love winter," she said. "It just goes on too long, so that by March I'm craving colors and flowers and leaves on the trees. Thanks, Liane, you're a darling. And you——" she looked up at Liane's companion "—must be Jake. Well ... Liane didn't tell me you're a knockout. How do you do?"

"Behave yourself, Megs," her husband said amiably, and shook Jake's hand. "Fitz Donleavy. Pleased to meet you; come on in and I'll make you a drink." He took Liane's coat and kissed her on the cheek. "As gorgeous as ever," he told her.

Liane grinned at Jake. "Discount at least half of what he says. And treat his curry with great respect."

Jake, who looked extremely handsome in tailored pants and a bulky sweater over an immaculate white shirt, smiled back. His smile hurt something in Liane, something she was not sure she could have defined. Although he was self-possessed and outwardly at ease, she wondered how often in the five years since his wife had left he had indulged in the kind of banter that was an integral part of the Donleavy household. Not often, she'd be willing to bet. Impulsively she tucked her arm in his as they went into the kitchen, where the wood-

90

stove sent off a comfortable heat and the air was redolent with spices. "Despite what I said, Megan and Fitz are my best friends," she added. "I met them in Charlottetown when Patrick was only a baby, and it was Fitz who found me the job with the Forsters. For which I remain everlastingly grateful."

Jake's wrist was tense under her fingers. Perhaps, Liane thought in a spurt of annoyance, he distrusted her motives in bringing him here. And perhaps he was right. Had she not hoped that if he met her friends he would be less judgmental of her? More ready to accept her at face value?

She moved away from him, lifting the lids of the saucepans on the stove and inhaling cautiously, determined not to let Jake ruin her evening. Giving one of the pots a stir, she laughed over at him. "I trust you're going to drive home...I have a feeling I may have to wash this down with a fair bit of wine."

"Just as long as I don't have to carry you into the house," Jake replied blandly.

She would like that, Liane thought, and said decorously, "In all the years I've known Fitz and Megan, I only once had to spend the night on the couch."

"That was when I made cranberry wine from my grandmother's recipe," Fitz chuckled. "You weren't the only one in trouble that night. My grandmother was a strict teetotaller, Jake—the wine was for medicinal purposes only, of course. To prevent the croup."

"I could have cleaned the drains with that wine," Megan said feelingly. "I hope you like curry, Jake."

"I spent the last four years in the Far East, during which I learned two things—to eat curry hot enough to peel the skin from the roof of your mouth, and not to inquire too closely as to what particular animal had ended up in the pot."

Fitz laughed. "Had I known that, I would have been more adventurous. Megan never lets me get too carried away when it's someone we haven't met before.. Whereabouts were you, Jake?"

Jake related some of his experiences in Thailand and Malaysia, after which Megan described a hair-raising adventure from her hitchhiking days in Turkey. The second bottle of wine was opened, the children were fed and the adults settled around the old oak table in the dining room. Liane was very happy. Jake fitted in beautifully with her friends, and was giving every appearance of enjoying himself; and how could he not, she thought, for it was one of those evenings when everyone seemed a little wittier than usual, when good fellowship flowed easily and laughter echoed around the table. Because she was happy, she flirted outrageously with Jake, egged on by Fitz, and none of it, she knew, was due to the wine.

The children were put to bed at eight-thirty, because there was school the next day. At one, the adults regretfully called it a night. "Patrick can stay if you like, Liane," Megan offered artlessly. "I'll get him off to school in the morning."

Liane would then be alone with Jake in the house. Very strenuously avoiding looking at him, she said, "He didn't bring his homework, and if he doesn't hand in his English assignment tomorrow he's going to be in deep trouble."

"Another time, then," said Megan. "You can carry Patrick, can you, Jake?"

"Sure," Jake replied with one of those fractional hesitations that Liane had noticed before. "I'll go and turn on the heaters in the wagon first."

When he came back in, blowing on his fingers to warm them, Liane led the way upstairs to Clancy's room. Patrick was sprawled on the old couch under the window, wearing his Edmonton Oilers tracksuit, fast asleep. "We'll wrap the blanket around him," she whispered.

Jake bent to gather the child into his arms while Liane adjusted the woolen folds of the blanket around Patrick's dangling limbs. Patrick muttered something fretfully, then burrowed his head into Jake's chest. For a split second the man looked as though someone had just skewered him with a knife; Liane's breath caught in her throat, but before she could say anything Jake's face had settled back into impassivity.

They went downstairs and said their goodbyes, then walked out into the cold, starlit night, the snow creaking under their boots. Liane climbed into her seat, and took Patrick from Jake, cuddling the boy to her chest, her chin resting on his auburn curls. They drove home in silence. Jake parked by the door, then walked around to take Patrick from her. "I'll carry him upstairs," he said briefly.

Patrick's homework occupied one half of the bed, his collection of hockey cards the other. "I wonder how much English did get done?" Liane murmured, clearing the stuff away and pulling the bedspread back. Jake laid the boy on the mattress, and Liane covered him up. Patrick opened his eyes, said distinctly, "The ref said it was for high-sticking," and closed his eyes again.

Although a half smile tugged at Jake's lips, his eyes were full of pain. Liane had drunk a considerable quantity of wine that night, and it was very late. Moving away from the bed, she said, "You must miss your son."

Jake's reaction, had she stopped to think, was entirely predictable. His fingers biting through her jacket, he took her by the elbow, hustled her down the stairs and yanked her around to face him in the hall. "How many times do I have to tell you to keep out of my private life?" he snarled.

Just so had her father looked when she had told him,
eight years ago, that she was pregnant. But Jake was not
her father. Liane planted her feet firmly on the carpet
and drew herself to her full height. "Private life, be
darned! What you're afraid of is being a human being.
With feelings and regrets and pain. You're the typical
macho male, the kind that Hollywood adores, all stiff
upper lip and suffering in noble silence. You're not a
man at all, Jake Brande—you're a robot!"

There was an instant's dead silence, while her words
echoed in her ears and she had the time to be horrified
that she had actually spoken them. "Oh, am I?" said
Jake, hauling her closer. "We'll see about that."

Liane knew instantly what he was going to do, and
knew too how wrong it would be. There had been enough
angry kisses between her and Jake. Too many. With the-
atrical eloquence she let her eyes roll back in their
sockets, her head flop forward, and her whole body go
as limp as Patrick's.

She was a small woman; but she was also a dead-
weight. Jake staggered a little, cursing under his breath
as he lowered her, more or less gently, to the floor. With
what she felt privately was great artistry, Liane lay very
still, feeling his knee dig into her spine and hearing
against her cheek the steady beat of his heart.

He said dryly, "It's okay, Liane—you've accomplished your purpose. You can come to now."

She sneaked a look at him through her lashes. "You
mean you weren't taken in?" she asked in an injured
tone.

"Most police officers get so they can recognize a
genuine faint when they see one."

She sat up, pushing her hair back from her face. "I
got second prize for acting at the finishing school I went
to in Switzerland."

"I believe every word of it. I'll drop my so-called macho image long enough to tell you that I wish to God I could tell when you're acting and when you're not."

"You think I'm acting all the time." Her forehead wrinkling in thought, speaking more to herself than to him, she went on, "I haven't needed to act since I left my father's house. I've learned to be myself instead ... funny, I hadn't realized that before."

His voice like a whiplash, Jake demanded, "So are you implying I'm like your father?"

Her leg was lying half across his as they crouched on the carpet, his face not six inches away from hers. It was, she decided, a very odd conversation to be having on the floor in the middle of the night. "No, you're not," she said thoughtfully. "The only emotion I ever get from my father is anger. I get anger from you, too. But I also see pain and laughter and gentleness." Her eyes suddenly danced. "But they're all rusty from disuse—that's it! You've put them all in cold storage, and now you're having a hard time making them work again."

"You're mixing your metaphors."

She had no idea what he was thinking, or whether every word she had said was nonsense. Unprompted, she rested her palm on his cheek, feeling the roughness of his beard and the heat of his skin. "I'm glad you're here," she said.

He took her uplifted hand in his own, staring at it as if he had never seen a woman's hand before, tracing the lines in her palm with one fingertip, then stroking the thin, capable fingers, bare of rings. Liane held her breath, the contact spreading from her hand through her whole body in waves as warm and full of color as a tropical sea. This was what she had wanted, she thought. This. Not a kiss fueled by anger.

Jake looked up, and the emotion in his eyes made the blood race in her veins. With exquisite gentleness he cupped her face in his hands and lowered his face to hers, his mouth drifting from her cheekbone down the smooth side of her cheek to find her lips.

Liane forgot about the carpet and the lateness of the hour. She felt as though she were swaying on a raft on the tropical sea, and the sea was beckoning her, beckoning her to slide into the silken warmth of depths that were unknown to her yet charged with fascination. She felt languorous and boneless; she also felt infinitely generous.

Their tongues met and played, a cave dance under the sea. Then Jake's hands slid beneath her jacket, finding the curve of her breast through her sweater, taking its fullness into his palm and caressing it. As sensation lapped at her, a rising tide impossible to hold back, Liane moaned with pleasure, and his kiss deepened.

Through his shirt she explored the taut, rounded muscles, probing with her fingers to learn what he felt like, this man who had come into her life so violently and so inevitably. But it was not enough. She hungered for the slide of flesh on flesh, for the removal of clothes that were in the way, barring her from truly knowing him.

As though he had read her mind, Jake raised his head, his eyes like smoldering coals. She saw him struggle to find a normal voice, and heard the hoarseness underlying it when he spoke. "You want me as much as I want you, don't you, Liane?"

"Did you ever doubt that?" she asked with a wobbly smile.

"I doubted it." He suddenly grinned at her, as carefree as a youth. "You seem to spend most of your time yelling at me."

"Sublimation."

"Ah..." Jake kissed her again, his lips brushing hers with an open sensuality that made her sway toward him. "We shouldn't be doing this. We have a business arrangement—you hired me, remember?"

"As a bodyguard," Liane said, twin devils of laughter sparking her eyes.

He said with all the intensity she could have wished for, "I don't want to guard your body—I want to possess it and put my mark on it and learn every inch of it."

It was exactly the way she felt about him. And perhaps because her face mirrored her thoughts, Jake said roughly, "Come to bed with me."

She wanted to. Oh, God, how she wanted to. But eight years ago life had taught Liane a hard lesson, and that lesson was still part of her. She said in a small voice, "I can't—I'm not protected against a pregnancy, Jake," and watched shock and surprise chase themselves across his face.

"I thought all women were nowadays."

"Not this one. I haven't had a lover since the man who fathered Patrick."

"*Eight years?*"

"That's right."

Jake eased his knee out from under her and flexed his thigh. "So why me?" he asked bluntly.

She spoke the literal truth. "I don't know."

"After eight years I should think anyone would do."

Liane's chin snapped up. "I've had the occasional date in those eight years. I have never once felt impelled to rip the man's clothing off and drag him to the nearest bed."

He gave a short laugh. "I'm flattered."

"You've gone away, Jake," she whispered. "What happened?"

"I don't know where I am with you," he said violently. "I just think I'm getting you figured out and you throw me for a loop again. *Eight years...*"

"I had a child to raise and a roof to put over our heads and money to earn—I didn't have the time or the energy to go chasing after everything in pants! Anyway, the only men I've really known have been my father, who I'm not sure has ever loved anyone, my brother, who was a carbon copy of Father, and Noel—who abandoned his own child without a thought. Why should I go chasing after another man? They're not that great!"

Liane scrambled to her feet, cold under her jacket, wishing once again that she had kept her mouth shut. Jake stood up with a lean grace that, upset as she was, still did funny things to her insides. "I don't like women and you don't like men," he said. "So why are we making love on the hall carpet at 2:00 a.m.?"

"You tell me," Liane answered irritably.

He chucked her under the chin. "Go to bed, Liane. Or you'll be even grumpier in the morning than you usually are."

"Don't patronize me!"

"What a little wildcat you are under that china-doll exterior. Good night...pleasant dreams."

He was openly laughing at her. Her body an ache of sexual frustration, her emotions churning like waves on a reef, Liane went to bed.

Monday morning. Monday mornings should never have been invented, Liane thought, tempted to throw the alarm clock at the wall as her feet hit the floor with a thud. She hauled her nightgown over her head, pulled on a tracksuit, and headed for the bathroom.

The living-room door was open. The sofa bed was neatly back in place, and Jake was on the floor doing push-ups. One right after the other, his back a long,

straight line, the muscles in his arms flexing in a way
that privately fascinated her. She said sharply, "You're
a masochist, Jacob Brande."

He glanced at her over his shoulder, not missing a
beat. His T-shirt, wet with sweat, clung to his spine, and
his forehead was slick with sweat. "Dressed already?"
he panted.

"Now that you've moved in I'll have to buy a
housecoat."

"I thought a housecoat was part of every woman's
wardrobe ... twenty-eight, twenty-nine, thirty. Phew!"
He stood up, bouncing on his bare feet and swiping at
his forehead with the back of his arm, his grin infec-
tious. "It's a lovely day, Liane; the sun's shining and
the sky's blue. Why don't you own a housecoat? Not
that you don't look very charming as you are."

She had made the mistake of wearing this particular
outfit to the greenhouse once, and the stains had never
come out. "All the housecoats I can afford are boring,"
she said obligingly. "Terry cloth and seersucker and in-
sipid pink satin. I want something exotic. An em-
broidered caftan or a silk sarong."

"You mean a caftan would make you spring out of
bed in the mornings full of *joie de vivre*?"

"I wouldn't guarantee that." Although right now she
was certainly full of sexual energy, which, while not quite
the same as *joie de vivre*, was for her most definitely a
new phenomenon. And one Jake was quite astute enough
to discern. She gave an exaggerated yawn, not realizing
how this made her breasts rise and fall under the loose
top. "Monday morning is the worst time of the week."

He advanced on her, his eyes dancing. "Perhaps we
could improve upon it."

His hair was clinging to his scalp, and something in
Liane that had been repressed for far too long leaped

up in response to the mischief in his face. "Just what would you suggest?"

Glancing down at his damp T-shirt, he said, "How about a little long-distance intimacy? Stand still, Liane."

Liane was not sure she could have done otherwise. Jake leaned forward and, as the laughter in his eyes flared into another emotion altogether, he found her mouth with his own.

He kept his hands at his sides, and made no move to close the gap between them, leaving all that he wanted to say to a kiss so sensual that Liane was lost in a haze of delight. She parted her lips to the gentle urgings of his tongue, to an exploration as intimate as any she had ever known; and she longed to disobey him, to step closer and wrap her arms around him and feel the hardness of his body press into the softness of hers.

Then he eased away from her. She opened eyes dazed with pleasure, unconsciously leaning toward him in an arc of hunger, and heard him say, "Does that improve the prospects of a Monday morning?"

"Immeasurably," Liane whispered, and was amazed that she could produce a sound at all, let alone a word of more than one syllable.

His gaze lingered on her flushed cheeks and tangled hair. "You don't look the slightest bit grumpy."

She said gravely, "Oh, I feel very grumpy. Because instead of doing what I want to do right now, I'm going to get Patrick up and go to work."

"I shall take that as a compliment."

"Certainly I withdraw any complaints I might once have made about your technique."

He flexed his muscles. "You ain't seen nothin' yet, babe."

Liane laughed, a lighthearted peal of laughter that Fitz would have approved of. "A whole new perspective on the first day of the week, and all before breakfast," she said, and took herself off to the bathroom.

She worked at the library all day, and that evening helped Patrick wrestle with a one-paragraph composition about dinosaurs. There was no recurrence of the kiss in the hallway. The next day she worked in the greenhouse. Jake was gone all day, returning only when Patrick got out of school; she did not inquire where he had been. But after an early supper she said to Patrick, "Would you like to go to Percy's this evening? Rosie had twins."

Despite his attachment to the vast reaches of the universe, Patrick also loved the clutter and the rich odors of Percy's farm. "Yeah!" he said. "Right now?"

"I'll give him a call to make sure he'll be home."

Percy's voice reverberated into the room; he would indeed be home. Liane looked across at Jake, who was still sitting at the table; he had treated her like a piece of furniture the last two days. "Percy is the owner of the manure spreader," she told him repressively. "You probably wouldn't want to come."

He raised an expressive brow. "I'll drive you in the wagon."

"Let's go, then," she said, rather ungraciously, and made sure she sat in the back seat on the way. But in the warm, hay-scented barn, where the cows shuffled in their stanchions and where Percy was so patently pleased to see them, Liane couldn't stay cross for long. The knobbly-kneed calves were as fascinated with Patrick as he was with them, there was a new crop of kittens in the feed room, and three dozen chicks peeping under an infrared bulb in one of the stalls. Their feathers were the soft yellow of marguerites.

Right behind her Percy boomed, "Glad to see you've made up with Jake—took to him right away last week."

He gave her a wink that distorted his whole face. "You need a man. All women do."

This, even for Percy, was somewhat heavy-handed. "Nonsense," Liane replied. "You men aren't nearly as indispensable as you like to think you are."

"Not right, you bringing up a boy on your own."

Liane flinched, for this was a direct hit. Jake interjected smoothly, "She's doing a great job, Percy. Tell me, what's your monthly milk yield?"

Another heavy-handed intervention, but it worked. Percy loved his dairy cows, and would discourse on butterfat and milk quotas for as long as he had an audience. Half an hour later they went to the farmhouse for tea, and then they drove home, Patrick chattering excitedly to Jake the whole way. Jake buried his nose in a book for the rest of the evening.

Liane worked in the library four more days that week because she needed the money, both to pay Jake and to add to the fund she had been saving for Patrick's March break; she had reserved a chalet in the Laurentians so that they could ski. As February blustered its way into March, and the days slowly lengthened, she sometimes wondered whether she had dreamed the encounter between her and Jake on the carpet in the middle of the night, or the salutary Monday-morning kiss in the hallway. Although he was pleasant and unfailingly polite to her, he was also as remote as the far shore of the river; the channel that had opened so briefly between them had frozen over.

She kept busy, determined that he not see that she was hurt. Gradually it became clear to her that she was acting again, playing the role of a cool, self-contained mother when she felt like someone quite different.

Certainly she was a mother; she had no problem with that. But cool? Self-contained? Whenever Jake walked in the room she breathed him in through every pore in her skin, and felt his physical presence pierce every nerve ending, as though her fingertips had been thrust into the blue heart of a flame. But his eyes were like doors shut tight against her, like stones unmoved by either her presence or her absence.

He had come close. He had retreated. She could understand neither the intimacy nor the separation. She could only ache with the loss of the closeness and yearn for its rebirth. And, because she was too proud to show her true feelings, she acted. She did not like this. But she did not know what else to do.

Midway through Jake's second week, Liane was standing at the kitchen counter one morning making Patrick's sandwiches for his school lunch when Patrick said, through a mouthful of cereal, "Is it okay if Jake takes me to hockey practice this evening, Mom?"

Wondering if she would have enough lettuce, she replied absently, "He always does."

"I mean just him and me. Not you."

Suddenly Patrick had her full attention. She flicked a glance at Jake, sipping his coffee and reading the paper, and saw this had not originated with him. "Why?" she asked blankly.

Patrick wriggled in his seat. "The other guys' dads take them," he said.

But Jake's not your father, she almost blurted out. Choosing her words, Liane said, "You'd like a man to take you?"

"Yeah. Just for today. Bobbie Graves, his dad always takes him, and he was teasing me 'cause I haven't got one."

She stared down at the bright green lettuce leaves, which she had grown herself. "Sure, that would be fine."

Patrick was not insensitive. "You don't mind, do you, Mom?"

It took every ounce of her fortitude to smile at him and say easily, "It's a great idea—I'll put my feet up and read for an hour... You'd better go and brush your teeth, Patrick; the bus will be here soon."

Patrick ran for the stairs, Jake rustled the newspaper, and through a sheen of tears Liane neatly wrapped the sandwiches in waxed paper. Patrick had never before told her that the boys teased him because he only had a mother, and she had always assumed he was quite happy that she was the one to take him to hockey. A tear plopped on the cookie tin as she lifted it out of the cupboard.

Jake's chair scraped on the floor. Dropping his hand on her shoulder, he said, "It had to happen sooner or later, Liane."

She jumped, and a cookie fell to the floor, chocolate chips shooting under the cupboard. Twisting to face him, her blue eyes anguished, she cried, "I've failed him—by not giving him a father."

"Don't be——" Patrick's steps thudded on the stairs. Jake added urgently, "Wipe your eyes, kiss him goodbye, and once I've seen he's safely on the bus we'll continue this."

She rubbed at her eyes, sniffing hard. "I have to be at the library at nine."

"You'll be five minutes late."

Liane quickly put an apple and the cookies in Patrick's lunch box, and bent to hug him. He and Jake left the kitchen. She knelt to clean up the cookie crumbs, and suddenly found herself leaning her forehead against the cupboard door and weeping, a great flood of tears she could not have stemmed for—for all her father's money, she thought dimly, and wept the harder.

She did not hear Jake come back in the room. She felt him take her by the shoulders, and with a sob buried her face in his chest, clutching him convulsively.

She cried for a long time. But eventually her tears ran out, as tears did, and she heard Jake say, "Here, blow your nose."

He put a box of tissues in her hand. She blew her nose, cleared her throat, and said, "I'm going to be more than five minutes late."

"I phoned them," he told her. "I told them you weren't feeling well but that you'd probably be in after lunch."

She looked at him through lashes stuck together in wet little clumps. "I can't go taking time off like that. I don't get sick leave because I'm only part-time, and I need the money—you're expensive."

"You don't have to pay me for this morning. Because you're going to put on a jacket and boots, and we're going to walk down to the river—both of us off duty."

There had been fresh snow in the night, the sun was streaming through the window, and Jake had just held her in his arms. "All right," Liane said.

"Docility—I don't believe it."

"I told you I was a good actress."

He reached out a hand to pull her to her feet. "So you did. Then tell me something—why do we always have these scenes at floor level?"

His fingers were warm as they curled around hers, and all the magic of his touch flowered instantly to life. Liane snatched her hand back. "Not that. Not right now."

"It's always there, though, isn't it?" Jake said slowly. "Every minute I'm in this house I'm aware of you."

"But you never touch me," she said with painful truth. "You haven't for days."

"I'm afraid to—didn't you guess that?" He grinned mirthlessly. "I can face a gang of drug bandits in the jungles of Thailand, but a woman who's five-feet-five has me on the run."

She eyed him warily, scrambling to her feet. "We're going for a walk," she reminded him. "Outdoors. After I wash my face."

Her face, in the bathroom mirror, looked exactly like that of a woman who had just cried her eyes out. Liane splashed cold water on it, and made no attempt to repair the ravages of too much emotion; let Jake see her as she was, she thought. The real woman. She was tired of acting. She pulled on her pink ski suit, which matched her pink nose, and went to join him at the back door.

CHAPTER EIGHT

IT WAS a beautiful day, the sun sparkling like flung jewels on the white carpet of snow, the sky as blue as Liane's eyes. She took a deep breath of the clean, cold air and was glad she wasn't buried in the stacks at the library, and even more glad that she was with Jake.

Truly with him. Jake, who was a man who kept his emotions tightly under wraps, had just admitted he was afraid of her. She needed time to think about that.

While they wandered down to the river she described what the gardens looked like in summer, her hands gesticulating, her face vivid with enthusiasm. The rhododendrons and azaleas, sheltered by tall pines, stood sturdily in the snow, their branches laced with long necklaces of crystals that sparkled more brightly than diamonds. The buds were tightly folded against the cold. "This one's called Snow in Summer," Liane said. "Pure white petals with just a touch of scarlet in the center."

"You know a lot about gardening."

"When Patrick gets a little older I'd like to take more courses on horticulture and landscape design...I love it."

They were emerging from the trees. Jake suddenly put a hand on her arm and whispered, "Look...to your left by the alders."

A red fox, his bushy tail brushing the snow, was loping across the field. As if he had sensed their presence, he stopped, testing the air with black nostrils, his ears pricked. Then with a great bound he headed for the tangle of shrubs, and disappeared.

"Wasn't he beautiful?" Liane breathed. "So wild and free..."

Jake said harshly, "Freedom's an illusion, Liane."

His words touched a chord she had secretly known was there, a raw place where resentment lingered. "That's easy for you to say. You've got a month's vacation, and you can decide to spend it here, there or anywhere. I love Patrick, but that love costs me my freedom. I'm not free—not like you!"

"You think I wouldn't trade what you've got for what I've got?"

"I would have thought you'd have spent your month off nearer your son," she said, and knew she had put into words the one facet of Jake's character she could not deal with.

The lines were scored deep into Jake's face. "I can't," he told her. "He's dead."

Into the silence a crow cawed somewhere over their heads, and from the riverbank another answered. "*Dead*?" Liane whispered.

"For four years."

She felt his pain as if it were her own, for how would she survive if something happened to Patrick? Jake was standing under a pine tree, his face in shadow; she closed the distance between them, stepping into the shadow to join him, and instinctively put her arms around him. But Jake struck her away. "Don't!" he said violently.

Keep your distance. Stay away. Without a trace of the emotion that was churning within her, Liane said, "Your wife left you five years ago...was your son living with you, Jake?"

He replied in the flat voice of one who had recited these facts before and had not allowed them to touch him. "No. I left him with her; I thought it was better that way—she was his mother. She remarried almost immediately, a decent enough guy, a lawyer with a nice, steady nine-to-five job. Five months later, after giving Daniel time to settle in, they went for a delayed honeymoon. I was going to take him for three weeks, but I had a case to tie up beforehand, so we'd arranged that he go to camp for a week... He fell out of a tree his fourth day there, and was dead by the time the other boys got to him.''

''And you've been blaming yourself ever since.''

''Wouldn't you?''

''Probably,'' she said honestly.

''My wife blamed me, too—or rather my job. She's had two children since then, both boys.''

''Whereas you left the country.''

''I applied for an overseas position, and when I got it I did my level best to get killed in the line of duty.'' Jake kicked at the snow with his boot. ''As you see, it didn't work. But, because I took every risk there was to take, I turned up drug cartels under every bush, and got myself promoted into the bargain. Two months ago head office pulled me out of there; it was getting a little too hot even for me, and that was when I realized I no longer wanted to end up six feet under the ground in the rain forest.'' He pushed away from the tree. ''I guess you could call that a cure of a kind.''

He was not cured at all, Liane thought, vaguely aware of how cold it was in the shade of the tree. ''I'm truly sorry I said that about freedom, Jake.''

''Loving Daniel was the closest I ever came to freedom,'' he revealed with painful exactitude. ''My wife and I fell out of love almost immediately. She'd married the glamorous police officer in the red serge uniform, and soon found out that there was precious little glamour in my job. I'd married a woman I'd thought was independent, and found her clinging to me night and day. But I loved Daniel. To use your words, I loved him more than anyone else in the world.''

Blinking back tears, Liane said, "I understand now why ever since you arrived you've been keeping your distance from Patrick."

Finally Jake reached out and touched her, his hand in its leather glove resting briefly on her pink sleeve. "If I find myself getting too fond of Patrick, I'll have to leave," he told her.

Feeling as though he had just punched her in the stomach, Liane said sharply, "And let him be kidnapped?"

"I don't think that's going to happen, Liane. Your father wouldn't court that kind of publicity—taking a child from its mother. Not in the circles he moves in."

The cold was penetrating to her very bones. "He knows what you seem to be blind to—that he has the power and I have none. No money, no influential friends. Only the vulnerability that comes from loving my son."

"I've been here nearly two weeks. Not a move. No sign of Chester—who could certainly have found you by now had he wanted to. I think you were exaggerating." Jake's voice gentled. "I understand why. But I don't believe Patrick's in jeopardy."

"Do you still think I'm trying to con my father?"

"I'm not quite so ready to believe that, either."

She should have been pleased by this admission; and she too had had moments of doubt about her father, for he was a man who moved fast when he wanted something, and as far as Patrick was concerned he had not moved at all. But she was neither pleased nor relieved. She moved back from Jake, not wanting him to see that she was shivering, and took refuge in anger. "Then if, according to you, Patrick's in no danger, maybe you're right and you should leave, Jake—before you risk loving someone again. Patrick. Or me. It doesn't really make any difference who, does it?"

His mouth a thin line, Jake snapped, "I said I'd stay for a month."

"I absolve you from that—you can leave any time you like. The sooner the better."

"I'll leave when I'm good and ready!"

"And what if Patrick gets attached to *you*? Have you thought of that? You saw what happened this morning—he could get hurt too, especially if he starts seeing you as a father figure."

Jake said tightly, "Yes, I'd thought of that."

He too had stepped into the sunlight. His eyes looked almost black to Liane, like the plumage of the crows cawing by the river. Seven crows a secret. Not stopping to think, because if she did she wouldn't say it, she went on, "I'm at risk, too. I'm in danger of falling in love with you, and I don't want to do that. So why don't you go home and pack your bags before anyone gets hurt—you or Patrick or me?"

He said flatly, "You have this gift for taking me by surprise—what do you mean, you're in danger of falling in love with me? It's called lust, Liane. Not love."

Liane retorted, grappling with a truth she had only just acknowledged, "I'll call it what I like. And love is the word I used."

"You don't like men—you said so."

With a faint smile she responded, "You're not men, Jake—I thought I'd made that clear to you. You're one particular man who affects me in a way I've never been affected before. I don't know if this is what falling in love feels like. I do know that it would be better for all of us if you left."

His eyes were like storm clouds at dusk, gathering in the blackness of the sky. "If we went to bed together, you'd understand what I mean when I talk about lust and love."

"Make love just to prove you right? No!"

"Make love for pleasure. For fun and laughter and sharing. But not for love."

To her dismay her whole body sprang to life. Almost inaudibly she said, "And then you'll get dressed and pack your bags and head off into the sunset? No, Jake, I won't do that."

"I'm not Noel!"

She glared at him across the snow. "I don't know who you are!"

She looked away, unable to bear the intensity of his gaze, and from the corner of her eye caught sight of the fox tracks, the paw prints close together where it had been trotting along, then abruptly separated by stretches of unmarked snow where it had bounded for the safety of the shrubs. It had known when to run, she thought, it was smarter than she was, and heard Jake say, "We talk too much, you and I. Let's go back to the house."

"We argue too much," she corrected. "We came out for a walk, and here we are fighting again."

"We wouldn't fight in bed," he said.

She bit her lip. She had no difficulty at all picturing herself and Jake lying naked side by side in her bed, his dark head cushioned on her breast, his strong thighs holding her close. She said frantically, "Stop it—I can't stand it!"

He ordered her pitilessly, "Go back to the house by yourself, then—and in the interests of compromise I'll stay until next week, when you and Patrick leave for the Laurentians."

Five more days. Pain constricted Liane's chest and tightened her throat. "Making love means just that," she asserted stubbornly. "Making *love*."

Deliberately ignoring her, Jake said, "You'll be working at the library until six tonight, won't you? I'll get Patrick's supper."

Five days. Then he would be gone, and she would never know if making love to him would have been different from the nights she had spent in Noel's cramped and not very clean apartment down by the waterfront. She was almost sure it would be different. Almost.

Inexorably her thoughts carried her forward. She had used the word risk a few moments ago; but how long since she had actually taken a risk?

Eight years ago, she thought. That was when she had come back from the protected environment of a very strict finishing school to go to university in Halifax. Drunk with freedom, she had gravitated to the art school crowd, fascinated by their repudiation of all the rules that had governed her life, enthralled by Noel, their flame-haired ringleader. Patrick had been the almost inevitable result.

Since then her whole life-style had mitigated against risk, especially where the opposite sex was concerned. Instead she had opted for noninvolvement. For safety. Risk she had banished along with all the untidy emotions that it could bring.

She took a deep breath and said steadily, "I've got a better idea, Jake. Let's go back to the house together and I'll show you what making love means to me."

Her words seemed to hang, frozen, in the crisp winter air; yet she had said them. Unquestionably she had said them. Dredging up all her self-reliance, she told herself that at least this way she would have memories when Jake was gone. Memories, and the satisfaction of knowing she had broken out of the shell she had built around herself so long ago.

Jake's whole body had gone very still. "Liane, do you mean that?"

She raised her chin. "Yes, I mean it."

"I'll protect you from pregnancy," he said.

She did not want talk of pregnancies; she wanted talk of love. And wondered if she was a fool to take this particular risk with this particular man, she who was not at all sure she knew what love between man and woman meant.

Then Jake said softly, "I've never faulted your courage."

Swinging her up into his arms, he began jogging through the pines, past the leather-leaved rhododendrons and out into the open space of the garden. Liane hung on, bouncing against his chest, feeling the strength of his arms and hearing his breath rasp in his throat. He took the back steps two at a time, and then he was pushing through the back door and locking it behind him, kicking off his boots as he did so.

Still holding her in his arms, he carried her to the door of her room. There he put her down. "I'll be back in a minute," he said. "Don't go away."

She knew where he was going: to get the protection he had mentioned. I'm crazy, she thought shakily. I'm doing exactly what I said I wouldn't do—having an affair with a man who's made it quite clear he doesn't love me now and won't hang around long enough to find out if he could love me in the future. This isn't risk. It's madness.

She was still standing rooted to the spot when Jake came back. He had shed his outer garments and was barefoot. Again he caught her up in his embrace, lifting her over the threshold and putting her down on the bed. Then he yanked off her boots and unzipped her snowsuit, all with a businesslike air that terrified her. "Jake——" she gasped. "Jake, I don't——"

He dropped the snowsuit to the floor, and lay down beside her on the bed, gathering her into his arms. "Don't look so worried, sweetheart," he said. "Maybe what you call making love and I call sharing is the same thing. Maybe we should just forget all the words and all the other people—Noel, and my wife and my son and yours—and do what seems the most natural thing in the world whenever we're together..."

Sweetheart, he had called her, he who was not a man to use endearments lightly. And the light in his eyes as he pushed her hair back from her face with hands that were not quite steady could very easily be construed as tenderness. Jake, I love you, Liane thought experimentally, and let the simple little words echo in her heart. Jake, I love you...

She had no idea whether she meant them or not; she did know she was glad to be where she was, lying beside him on the bed, that it was where she had wanted to be for what seemed like a very long time. She smiled into his eyes. "I think you've got the right idea. No talk..."

"No arguments," he added, laughter lines fanning from the corners of his eyes.

"No past or future," she went on seriously. "Just the present."

"Here and now, you and me. Show me how you'd make love to me, Liane."

His voice had a note she had not heard before, and his face was unguarded, gentle in a way that was new to her. Perhaps here in her bed she would learn more about Jake than about herself, she thought, taking his face between her palms and kissing him. The first touch of her lips was shy, tentative, poised for flight, because she was, at some level, still afraid. But his mouth was warm and familiar to her, and very much desired, so that she found nothing to frighten her and everything to encourage her. As he threw his thigh over her legs, just as she had imagined he would, she dropped her hands and started undoing the buttons of his shirt one by one.

He leaned up on one elbow, watching her, his eyes intent on her face. She glanced up, her lips a warm curve, her face open to him and without guile. When he kissed her, a slow, sensual kiss, she lost track of the buttons and instead ran her fingers through the dark hair that covered his chest, and then clasped his rib cage, exulting in the hard curve of bone and the heat of his skin. With a tiny ripping sound the last button gave way.

Against her mouth Jake said, "You did once mention tearing my clothes off, didn't you?"

She chuckled. "I hadn't realized I was so literal-minded."

And then she said nothing for quite a while, as Jake lifted her shirt over her head and unclasped her bra, tossing the garments to the floor and taking the fullness of her breasts in his hands. A few minutes later his shirt joined hers, and then two pairs of jeans and two sets of underwear.

They were facing each other on the bed, the clear winter sun falling impartially on them both as Jake's hands ran the length of her body from her shoulders down the pale slope of her breasts to the slim, neat waist and the stretch marks on her belly. He said huskily, "Every night since I've met you I've lain awake in the middle of the night and tried to picture your body... I never imagined it could be this beautiful." His face was suddenly full of doubt. "I'm afraid I'll hurt you, you're so small and delicately made..."

Intuitively Liane knew that it was his wife, the woman who had never accepted Jake as he was, who was responsible for his doubts. Fiercely she said, "I'm tough, Jake. I've borne a child, remember? And I want you so much I don't see how you could possibly hurt me." She reached out a hand, wrapping it around all the hardness that was his need for her, and saw his face convulse with longing.

He said jaggedly, "It's been so long...oh, God, come here, Liane."

She met him more than halfway, and their first coupling was fast and primitive and strong, over almost before it had begun. But even as Jake lay across her, panting, his hand was smoothing the length of her thigh and the rise of her hip, and without haste he started kissing her again, slow kisses of exploration and burgeoning desire. And again Liane met him more than halfway, letting him see her own hungers, guiding him to touch her where she was most sensitive, finding what pleased him and giving with measureless generosity and obvious pleasure.

The second time was like the gradual opening of a summer flower to the sun, and, as the golden heat enveloped her and the flames pulsed within her, Liane clutched Jake to her with all her strength, hiding from him neither the broken cries coming from deep in her throat nor her passion-dazed eyes. She saw his face clench, felt his own throbbing as if it were her own, and buried her face in the hollow of his shoulder, loving him with all her heart.

He collapsed beside her on the bed, his chest heaving, holding her as if he never meant to let her go. Feeling utterly safe, a safety she was not sure she had known since the long-ago days when her mother had held her, Liane said, "Do you know what?"

Jake raised his head, his eyes suddenly full of laughter. "I couldn't begin to guess."

She ran her fingertip along the entrancing dip of his collarbone. "This all felt so natural," she murmured. "As though we've been doing it together for years...do you know what I mean?"

He nodded. "Is that new for you?"

"Oh, yes." Her forehead wrinkled. "I was paralyzingly shy with Noel, and it was always awkward, jumpy, full of fits and starts. And in the end I never quite felt the way I thought I should—I was often disappointed, and yet the fault had to be in me; Noel seemed to think everything was fine."

In a carefully noncommittal voice Jake asked, "And today was different?"

Liane's smile was lilting. "You're fishing for compliments, Jake Brande! You know darn well it was different. I never knew I could be so—so swept up, so completely taken over." She gave a sigh of repletion, nuzzling at his throat. "It was wonderful."

He hesitated, and she felt the tension in the arm lying across her. "It was different for me, too. You gave me more than I've ever been given. Freely. Because you wanted to."

His wife had not been like that; Liane knew she had not. She said simply, "I didn't even think about giving— I just did what felt right, and loved every minute of it."

She had used the word love. And could use it again, she thought slowly. Could say to him, Jake, I love you, and know the words for the truth. She scanned his face, letting her eyes dwell on every detail, so well-known to her, so dearly loved, and heard him say harshly, "When you look at me like that, I—hell, I don't know what I'm saying. It hurts, Liane. Hurts something so deep that I scarcely know it's there."

She held her breath. "Tell me about it."

He shook his head, running his fingers through his hair. "It's nothing; I'm being a fool..." With an effort she could actually see, he banished the shadows from his face. "If you're going to work this afternoon, you'd better get moving, lady. It's eleven forty-five."

She sat up, gaping at the clock by the bed. "It can't be! Already?"

"That's what happens when you're having fun," Jake said, leering at her as he buried his face between her breasts.

She giggled, pushing him away. "Stop that! How am I going to face Miss Mablethorpe at the library after doing what we've just done? It must be written all over me."

Jake scanned her flushed cheeks. "Tell her you've got a fever," he suggested. "Maybe she'll send you home to recuperate."

"Maybe she'll send me down to the basement to unpack books," Liane countered. "I won't even have time for lunch."

Jake's grin was frankly lascivious. "I thought I'd already given you lunch...but, if you insist, I'll make you a sandwich."

Liane made a face at him, bounced out of bed and started grabbing clothes from her closet. "Peanut butter and cheese spread," she said promptly.

Jake raised an expressive eyebrow. "You'd prefer *that* to me?"

Liane turned, a skirt and blouse draped over her arm, and fluttered her lashes coyly. "Oh, I wouldn't go that far."

"How about some black olives on the cheese spread?" he asked, getting out of bed and stretching with a muscular grace that made her wish Miss Mablethorpe on the other side of the continent.

"I wouldn't go that far, either," she replied, and fled to the shower.

She got to work with two minutes to spare, two minutes that Jake spent very comprehensively kissing her goodbye, and sneaked in the side door of the library. Miss Mablethorpe was undoubtedly related to the head nurse in her moral standards if not by ties of blood, and

would be genuinely scandalized were she to suspect just
how Liane had spent the morning.

Fortunately Miss Mablethorpe was still on her lunch
break. Liane settled herself with a pile of new orders
and began cataloging them, although she did have a
tendency every little while to gaze off into space with a
tiny smile on her lips. Jake had been wonderful—the
kind of lover that subconsciously she had always
dreamed of, and now that they had crossed the bridge
into true intimacy she did not think there would be any
more talk of his leaving. Only when she remembered the
pain that had surfaced in his eyes, a pain he had refused
to talk about, would a frown cloud her face.

The afternoon seemed to last forever. At five to six
Liane put the pile of cards on her boss's desk, and said
good-night. Miss Mablethorpe, who had probably never
told a lie in her life, smiled at her trustingly. "Good
night, Ms. Daley. I'm glad you're feeling better."

Liane fought down a blush and escaped to the outdoors. The red wagon was parked on the street, Jake at
the wheel, Patrick and all his hockey gear in the back.
Jake said casually, "I'll drop you off at home, Liane,
and we'll go on to the practice."

She had forgotten about the hockey practice; yet that
was what had started everything. Jake drove off, his attention on the road, his ungloved hands resting lightly
on the wheel. She thought of some of the things those
hands had done to her, shivered with secret pleasure,
and turned in the seat so that she could see Patrick.
"How was your day?" she asked, and was surprised to
hear that her voice sounded quite normal.

He gave her a gleeful grin, his red hair sticking out
like the halo of an unruly saint. "I made a hundred in
math and thirty-three less in English," he said.

Liane did some quick calculations in her head based
on the last test. "Thirty-three is better than forty-three."

"That's what I thought . . . Bobbie'll be surprised to see me at hockey with Jake. Jake's gonna referee the game—the coach asked him to."

"I used to play Junior A hockey," Jake interjected, turning down the driveway.

He had yet to look her in the eye. Suddenly frightened out of all proportion, feeling exiled from far more than a hockey practice, Liane reached for the door handle. "Have fun, Patrick," she said with a lightness she was far from feeling.

Jake briefly touched her on the shoulder. When her eyes flew to meet his she was rewarded with a smile of singular sweetness that made her long to throw her arms around him and never let him go. "See you later," he said.

It was not often that Liane wished Patrick a thousand miles away, but right now she did. "Okay," she replied, and slid to the ground. The wagon drove away. She went in the house.

In the kitchen a hearty stew was bubbling on the stove, the vegetables were prepared, and on the table in an exquisite crystal vase that she had never seen before was a single deep red rose. The base of the vase was resting on a small envelope. Liane opened it. In a decisive and very masculine scrawl Jake had written, "Thank you for this morning. You more than proved your point. Jake."

Liane sat down in the nearest chair, inhaled the elusive scent of the rose, and wondered why, when she was so happy, she should feel like crying.

CHAPTER NINE

WHEN Jake and Patrick returned, Liane had the kitchen cleaned up and was sitting in the living room knitting, having discovered she could not concentrate on a book. Patrick dashed in the room and flung his jacket on the nearest chair, his hair plastered to his forehead where he had perspired under his helmet. "We had a practice game and the coach put me on forward and I got two goals," he announced. "Bobbie got three penalties, didn't he, Jake?"

"Two for icing, one for roughing."

"It was fun," Patrick said with immense satisfaction. "Will you take me again next week, Jake?"

"You'll be on your school break next week," Jake replied evasively.

"Oh, yeah . . . are you coming with us? Is he, Mom?"

Liane opened her mouth with no idea what she was going to say. Jake put in smoothly, "No, I can't come, Patrick."

Patrick's face fell. "We're going skiing in the Laurentians—I bet you're a good skier. Why can't you come?"

Quickly Liane said, "Jake's reasons could be private, Patrick; you mustn't pry."

Staring at Jake, Patrick said rebelliously, "But you'll be here when we get back, won't you?"

Jake knelt beside him, clasping the boy by the shoulders. "I don't know. Your mother hired me to keep an eye on you because of the threats that your grandfather made. But it's beginning to look as though he

122

didn't mean them, and I can't stay too much longer—I have a job to go to up in Ottawa."

Patrick's lower lip quivered ominously. "Why don't you marry my mom, and then we could all stay together?" he blurted.

One of Liane's knitting needles slid to the floor and she dropped six stitches. She had been afraid that her son would get too fond of Jake, and she had been right. Jake said soberly, "I understand how much you'd like that, Patrick, but your mother and I can't make that kind of commitment just because you want us to."

"Don't you like her?" Patrick demanded, glowering at the man hunkered down in front of him.

"Of course I do. But there's more to marriage than liking someone."

Patrick's gray eyes flooded with tears that spilled over and began to stream down his cheeks. "I don't want you to go!" he wailed, and threw himself into Jake's arms. Jake staggered under the weight, bracing himself as he hugged the boy to his chest, his mouth set and his eyes grim. Liane said nothing, her stomach curdling with fear. What was it Jake had said? If I find myself getting too fond of Patrick, I'll have to leave...

Although Patrick cried only rarely, he did a thorough job when he did cry. Jake's jacket was blotched with tears when the boy finally pushed himself away, his nose red and his eyes still watery. "I'm going upstairs," he muttered, and ran from the room.

Unable to bear the look on Jake's face, for the last boy he would have held like that must have been his own son, Liane bent and picked up the needle and then got to her feet. "I'll go and see if he's all right," she said.

"Leave him, Liane."

Jake had levered himself upright, and was picking Patrick's coat up from the chair. "He's upset," she told him unnecessarily.

"And you can't make it better. So don't try."

In a voice she strove to make casual, Liane asked, "Won't you be back after the break?"

"After what just happened, you should be begging me to stay away," he said grimly.

In the same even voice she heard herself ask, "You wouldn't give any thought to marrying me?" and as soon as the words were out wished them unsaid, for the look on Jake's face gave her her answer.

"You're the one who said no past and no future, only the present."

He was right, of course. She had. Abruptly she headed for the door, giving him a wide berth. She need not have bothered; he made no attempt to stop her.

Patrick was curled up in a ball on his bed. Liane sat down beside him, inwardly praying for wisdom. "Why don't you get into bed and I'll bring you up some cookies and milk?"

"Not hungry."

"I'll leave them by your bed, then, in case you want a midnight snack."

Patrick lifted his face; because he was fair-skinned, there were blue shadows under his eyes. "I bet if you asked him to marry you, he would," he burst out. "It's okay for girls to ask—our social studies teacher said so."

The social studies teacher was an ardent feminist. Wishing she could find this funny, Liane said, "I'm afraid you're wrong, Patrick. To Jake we're just part of a job he took on. And now he doesn't think the job needs doing any more. So he'll be leaving very soon." Maybe if she said this often enough she'd begin to believe it herself.

"I hate him!" Patrick cried, tears spurting over his lashes again.

Knowing better than to debate this, Liane said firmly, "That's enough, love. Hop into bed and I'll bring you up the cookies."

When she went downstairs there was a note on the hall table in handwriting she now recognized. "Gone for a walk. J." Risk, she thought bitterly, smoothing the scrap of paper in her hands. After today, she would never take another risk in her life.

Patrick had calmed down by the time she went upstairs with the cookies and milk; she read to him until she saw his lashes drift to his cheek and his head fall sideways on the pillow. Then she switched out the light and went back downstairs.

There was no sign of Jake. Liane soaked in a tub filled to the brim with hot water, picked up the dropped stitches and knitted several rows on her sweater, and went to bed, closing the door behind her. An hour later she was still wide-awake, staring into the darkness, when she heard the soft opening and closing of the front door and then the squeal of the hinges as Jake pulled out the sofa bed. He went to the bathroom. The bedsprings creaked as he lay down. And eventually she must have gone to sleep.

Liane woke at one and at two-thirty and at twenty to four, and each time she lay with burning eyes praying for sleep so that this interminable night would be over. Normally she hated mornings. But tonight she found herself longing for the arrival of dawn, which couldn't possibly be worse than the agonizing slowness of these hours of darkness.

When she saw her bedroom door open and heard a voice whisper her name, she almost thought it was part of a dream; certainly it did not occur to her to be frightened. She half sat up, pushing her hair back from her face. "Jake? Is that you?"

Jake came through the door, then closed it behind him. He was wearing a pair of jeans, the hair on his chest a dark blur. Leaning against the door, he said in a voice gravelly with exhaustion, "I couldn't sleep. You were awake, too."

She hugged her knees under the covers, almost dizzy with happiness that he was here in her room. She nodded, not trusting herself to speak.

"I should stay away from you," he rasped. "Stay away and get the hell out of here in the morning."

"Don't talk that way!" she cried. "I hate it when you do."

He said, speaking so low she had to strain to hear him, "I want you so badly I don't know myself any more—don't know why I'm here or what I'm doing or where I am...you're the only reality. The perfume of your body. Your incredible generosity. Your——" he hesitated, searching for the words "—beauty of soul."

Liane said quietly, for those last three words were the kind of words she had wanted from him for what seemed like forever, "Come here, Jake."

He was still standing by the door, his eyes like black holes in his face. She reached down, pulled her nightgown over her head and tossed it to the floor, then held her arms out to him, her breasts a pale gleam in the darkness. With a muffled groan Jake crossed the distance between them, like an arrow flying to the gold. He fell on top of her, wrapping his arms around her with crushing strength, holding her as if he never meant to let her go. Her nostrils were filled with the scent of his body, her nipples rasped by the mat of hair on his chest, and again she felt that dizzying surge of happiness. "I want you too," she whispered. "Oh, Jake, I want you so much..."

The words were almost banal, but not the intensity with which she spoke. Jake raised his head and kissed her, an impassioned kiss full of desperation and hunger, and somehow she caught the mood from him. They made love in silence, claiming each other with a raw honesty and pride that made a mockery of both modesty and inhibition, and that allowed no barriers between them. He rode her like a wild stallion, and frantically she gathered him in, arching her back, her own rhythms galloping through her body, carrying her to the very brink of the cliff and the long plunge into an oblivion that was balanced on the knife edge between pleasure and pain.

Jake collapsed beside her, and they lay still, their limbs entangled and hearts racing, and Liane could not have separated her own panting breath from his. She did not want to, she thought muzzily. She didn't ever want to be separated from him.

As if someone had pulled a black curtain over her eyes, she fell asleep.

Liane woke to the pallor of a winter dawn and to Jake's hand edging itself from under her breast. Rubbing at her eyes, feeling once again how natural it was to wake and find him there, she wrapped her arms around his ribs and said contentedly, "Good morning. I didn't dream you after all."

With a thread of laughter in his voice Jake replied, "For dreams like that you could be arrested."

She smoothed her palm over the crest of his hipbone to his thigh. "You feel so nice," she murmured. "Did we really do some of the things that I remember us doing?"

"And more," assured Jake.

"Well," said Liane.

He kissed the tip of her nose. "It's five to seven and I'd better get out of here before Patrick wakes up."

She groaned. "You mean I have to get up and make his lunch and go to work? Maybe that's why I'm such a grump in the mornings...because I'd rather be in bed with you." And, her eyes brimming with mischief, she did something very suggestive with her free hand.

The response raced across Jake's face. "You're a temptress. A siren. I'm going to put the coffeepot on."

But for a moment he stayed where he was, resting on his elbow, drinking in the pale beauty of her body. Liane said shakily, "When you look at me like that I can hardly breathe."

"I know the feeling." He smiled at her, a smile that made her heart turn over with love. "You look like the cat that ate the canary...a rather tired cat, at that."

"A substantial canary," Liane added demurely.

He laughed. "Wipe the grin off your face—Miss Mablethorpe will know exactly what you've been up to."

He climbed out of bed, and Liane watched as he pulled on his jeans, admiring the long line of his spine and the smooth play of muscles in his back, already feeling the emptiness in her arms where she had been holding him. From the bedside table the alarm began to beep.

Her feet hit the floor. "*That* takes the grin off," she announced, and yawned, stretching her arms over her head, her naked body silvered by the pale morning light.

Jake had been standing by the door, his hand on the knob. He said in a voice raw with feeling, "I can never get enough of you...right now I'd give everything I own to be able to spend the morning in bed with you."

Fear brushed her like the wings of a moth that dwelt in the dark, for the emotion in his voice had not been pleasure but a kind of baffled resentment. She picked up her nightgown and pulled it over her head. "I've got to have a shower, Jake."

"Yeah..." He was looking at her almost as if she were an enemy; she scurried past him and locked herself in the bathroom. Her eyes, like Patrick's last night, were blue shadowed. Scowling at her reflection, she reached for her toothbrush and tried to submerge her confusion in the routine of an ordinary weekday morning.

Patrick looked tired, and at the breakfast table spoke to Jake as little as possible. Liane kissed him goodbye, and watched him trudge up the hill to catch the school bus, his boots scuffing in the snow. How had Jake so swiftly found his way through their defenses? she wondered helplessly.

Because Patrick wants a father. And because I was ready to fall in love.

The big yellow bus pulled up at the top of the hill, and Patrick climbed aboard. Although Liane was sure he wasn't watching, she waved anyway. Then she went indoors to make her own lunch, after which Jake drove her to the library. "Patrick and I will pick you up at six," he said. "Don't shelve the As under Z, will you?"

"Jake, I——" She stopped, frustrated, wondering if all love affairs were so difficult, so fraught with undercurrents, knowing in a way that she was glad to have a few hours away from him. "I won't," she told him, and despite herself leaned over to kiss him goodbye. Their lips met and fused as if the wild coupling in the night had never happened. She pulled back and said unhappily, "I wish I knew what was going on."

"I'll do my best not to hurt you—I swear that. And I promise I'll be here tonight."

Tonight, yes. But what about tomorrow and the next day and the next?

At four o'clock Miss Mablethorpe beckoned Liane to the telephone, her lips pursed. "A personal call, Ms. Daley," she said, passing the receiver across her desk. Personal calls were frowned upon in the county library.

"Hello?" said Liane.

"It's Megan. Patrick got off the bus here, says he wants to stay the night. Is that okay with you? It's fine with us."

Liane knew instantly why Patrick wanted to be at Megan's: so he wouldn't have to deal with Jake. Her heart sank, for how could she blame him? Horribly aware that her boss was listening to every word, she said, "Jake says he's leaving on Monday... that's the problem."

"I rather thought so. Fitz says there are ways you could change his mind."

"Tell Fitz to get lost."

"Jake *can't* leave, Liane—he's perfect for you!"

Liane was in complete agreement. Perhaps her silence spoke for itself; Megan added, "He could go with you to the Laurentians, couldn't he?"

"Patrick already asked him—he doesn't want to."

Megan said something very pungent that Liane hoped Miss Mablethorpe had not overheard. "Do you want me to speak to him? Jake, I mean."

"No! Megan, I've got to go. Tell Patrick to let Jake know where he is. And phone me if Patrick changes his mind this evening and wants to come home."

"Will do. Good luck—he's such a *fool*!" And Megan hung up.

She had not been referring to Patrick. Liane replaced the receiver, gave Miss Mablethorpe a vague, unhappy smile, and went back to the stacks. She would have approximately fourteen hours alone with Jake in the house. Fourteen hours to change his mind.

But how?

Jake's opening words as Liane climbed in the wagon were, "Patrick's staying at Megan's."

"I know. She phoned me."

"You don't think he should be home on a school night?"

She raised her chin in deliberate challenge. "Tomorrow's the last day of school before the break. And if you're still planning to leave on Monday, what's the point of him seeing more of you than he has to?"

"Patrick's the crux of the matter, isn't he?" Jake banged his clenched fist on the wheel in frustration. "Liane, if this were just a question of you and I, two adults, I'd probably stay. But it isn't. There's a seven-year-old boy involved, a boy who's crying out for a father and who's incapable of hiding his feelings. If you and I got involved and it didn't work out—sure, we'd get hurt, but we could handle it. But I can't risk that with Patrick! I won't!"

She could see the tension bunched in his fists, taut in his jawline. "Because your own son's dead," she said.

Staring straight ahead of him through the windshield, Jake said tightly, "I wasn't always a perfect parent—who is? And now that Daniel's dead I can't make amends...but what I can do is not mess up Patrick's life."

When she touched Jake on the arm she could feel the tremors running through his body. Acting on instinct, she took him by the shoulders, saw the tears blurring his eyes, and drew him close, her heart aching for him.

His head sagged onto her shoulder and she felt a hard, dry sob shake him, the pent-up emotion of a man who had never given himself permission to cry. Holding him close, Liane let her cheek drop on to his hair, so thick and clean and soft.

The library door opened and Miss Mablethorpe came out, carefully locking it behind her; she never trusted anyone else with this task. Then she walked down the path toward the wagon. From her perspective she would have seen a furtive embrace in the front seat of a car on the premises of her beloved library. Liane, glaring at her over Jake's head, dared her to do anything about it.

Head in the air, Miss Mablethorpe scurried past the wagon, got in her little brown two-door, and drove off with an unladylike clash of gears. Greatly heartened by this small victory, Liane rubbed her cheek in Jake's hair and murmured, "If men could cry more and women could yell more, we'd all be a lot better off."

Slowly he freed himself, making no effort to hide the tears streaking his face. "But real men don't cry..."

"And nice girls don't get angry."

"It does seem kind of ridiculous, doesn't it? Maybe if I'd let out some of the emotion clogged up inside me after Daniel died, I wouldn't have tried so damn hard to walk in front of a stray bullet out in Thailand."

Liane said forcefully, "I'm very glad you didn't succeed."

"So, right now, am I. Who walked past a moment ago?"

She should have known he wouldn't have missed that. "My boss. She undoubtedly thinks that by now we're fornicating on the floor of the wagon."

"Between the brake pedal and the clutch... it would have the charm of novelty, Liane."

She loved it when he smiled like that. "I'm ten years too old," she insisted.

"Somehow I doubt that." He brushed her lips with his. "Thanks," he said. "Shall we go home?"

When she walked in the door there was a stack of mail on the hall table, including a large flat box neatly wrapped in brown paper, the return address a street in Ottawa she had never heard of. Jake said with unusual awkwardness, "It's from me—something I had at home that I asked the housekeeper to send here."

She gave the box a little shake. "You mean it's a present?" Jake nodded. Her face lit up, almost as Patrick's would have. "What is it?" she asked, starting to tear at the paper as impatiently as a child.

"It's not—well, you'll see."

The parcel had been thoroughly taped. Liane ripped at it, lifted the lid of the box and pushed aside the tissue paper. A length of raw silk lay in the box, gleaming dully, its shade somewhere between turquoise and blue. She shook it out, holding it against her in front of the hall mirror. "It matches my eyes," she marveled. "Is it from Thailand?"

"Yes...I bought it because I loved the color." He hesitated. "It's almost as though I knew I'd meet you."

"I could make a housecoat out of it—a caftan." She shook out the rest of the fabric, swatching herself in it and admiring her reflection. "Jake, it's beautiful—thank you so much."

Her eyes were brilliant, her cheeks flushed with pleasure. Jake said hoarsely, "Come to bed with me, Liane. Now."

She clutched the fabric to her breast and met his eyes. "It's where I've wanted to be all day," she told him.

He led her into the room, tossed the material on the bed, and began undressing her, his face intent, his movements deliberate, as if he had all the time in the world. When she was naked, he lifted her on the bed, so that she lay in a tangle of blue silk, her skin like ivory, her irises catching all the hidden fire of the fabric. "I'd like a painting of you like that," he said huskily, unbuttoning his shirt and throwing it over the chair. Liane lay still, her limbs heavy with desire, and watched him take off his clothes, wondering if she would ever have enough of him, this dark-eyed man so well-known to her yet still so much a stranger.

They made love with the same deliberate intensity with which Jake had undressed her, in utter silence, as though they could trust their bodies to say all that needed to be said. Afterward Liane drifted into a light sleep, waking to find that Jake had switched on the lamp by the bed and had been watching her sleeping face. She smiled at him drowsily, admiring the play of light and shadow on his face. "You look very serious," she said.

"Trying to figure you out," he replied with a lightness that did not quite ring true.

She answered with the same lightness, "What you see is what you get."

"You're an enigma to me," he burst out. "A mystery."

Unconsciously her muscles tensed. He was lying just far enough away from her so that she lacked the courage to touch him. "No mystery, Jake. I'm an ordinary woman who had an illegitimate child and who's been trying ever since to cope as best she can."

She was not sure he even heard her. "Since I was just a kid I thought I had women taped," he said in a stony voice. "They were the leavers and the takers. My mother left my father when I was four. She'd fallen in love with an Italian count who didn't like children, so she left me behind and never once visited me. For the next twelve years, which is when I left home, my father had a series of mistresses. He'd lavish expensive gifts on each one until she bored him, then out she'd go, and along would come the next one. Grasping women, greedy women, out for all they could get, women who would either sneer at the word love or who would look at you with total incomprehension, so far was it from their experience. My father, you understand, is a very rich man. Richer than yours."

Jake drew a ragged breath, and his eyes, lost in the past, slowly took note of the woman lying beside him on the bed. "I never meant to tell you this," he said irritably. "I don't know why I am."

The aura of safety in which Liane had fallen asleep was gone, for Jake's face was the face he had shown her in the schoolhouse when they had first met: closed, angry, and guarded. She propped herself up on her elbow and said strongly, ticking off her points one by one, "I'm not like your mother—I'd never leave Patrick! Neither am I one of your father's mistresses. I don't want your money, or my father's. You're a highly intelligent man—intelligent enough to know that all women aren't like them."

His eyes were like flecks of obsidian. "My wife, who I thought was different, was like them. Once she figured out life as a police officer's wife wasn't the bed of roses she'd expected, she left me, got the biggest settlement she could out of the courts, and then blamed me when Daniel was killed."

"I'm not her, either," Liane blazed. She sat up, searching vainly for something to cover herself other than the crushed length of silk. "I'm tired of feeling as if I'm on trial for crimes I've never committed. For heaven's *sake*, where's my nightgown?"

"You're not on trial! I'm trying my damnedest to trust you."

"It's called risk, Jake," she said tempestuously. "You can take the risk of trusting me, or you can drive off to Ottawa on Monday morning congratulating yourself on what a narrow escape you had. But you can't play it both ways. Because it hurts too much."

Her voice had cracked. Furious with herself, she got out of bed and began gathering up her clothes, pulling them on any which way. She was buttoning her blouse on the wrong buttons when Jake's hand fell on her wrist. "I'm learning to trust you, Liane—I swear I am. It's just—this has all happened so fast. It's not even three weeks since we met each other, and I never in my life expected to be affected by a woman the way you affect me." He managed a smile. "I'm still reeling from the shock."

She had had some of the same feelings herself. In a small voice she conceded, "I guess I shouldn't have lost my temper."

"It cleared the air," he said wryly. "Here—your blouse is crooked."

His fingers brushed her breasts as he fumbled with the tiny buttons. His attention on them rather than on her, he said, "I need to go to Ottawa next week—there's some business I have to deal with, and I have to see my boss at headquarters. But if you like, I could come back."

She swallowed. "Yes, I'd like that."

He glanced up. "Sweetheart, don't cry..."

"It's b-because I'm happy."

He put his arms around her, holding her wordlessly, and in the warmth of his embrace Liane indeed felt happiness well up within her, golden as the sun. He would come back. He trusted her, and he would come back. He had promised he would. So she did not need to tell him that she loved him; there would be time for that.

Time, she thought, dizzy with joy, wondering if there had ever been a more beautiful word in the whole language. Time for trust to build. Time for love...

CHAPTER TEN

LIANE had no idea how long she and Jake stayed locked together in the middle of the room. Her face was radiant when she finally looked up, although her words were prosaic. "We haven't had any supper," she said.

"Put on your best dress and I'll take you out."

"I could wrap myself in blue silk."

"I wouldn't be able to keep my hands off you. Mind you, I may not be able to anyway."

The expression on his face made her heart skip a beat. "It's our first proper date."

He looked over at the tumbled sheets. "Past due, I'd say."

An hour later, in the formal dining room of one of the city's hotels, they were sipping wine and eating mussels broiled in garlic butter. Liane was wearing her favorite color—a rose pink dress made of the finest wool, and her face glowed with happiness. Jake, in smart pants and a blazer, looked subtly different from the man she was used to in blue jeans; but the expression in his eyes was well-known to her, and made her heart sing. She ate salad and medallions of pork and fresh California strawberries, and all the while at the back of her mind was the thought that she and Jake could spend the night together—a whole night in her bed, in an intimacy that did not preclude sex but that somehow went beyond it.

They lingered over coffee and liqueurs, and when they finally left the dining room Liane gave it a last glance over her shoulder, knowing she would always remember how happy she had been this evening, certain that this

was the first of many such evenings to be spent with
Jake.

When they got home, Liane unlocked the front door,
and the warmth and silence of the empty house enfolded
them. Jake tossed her fur mittens on the hall table, inadvertently knocking the pile of letters to the floor as
he did so, and took her in his arms, kissing her very
tenderly. "We could go to bed," he said. "We might
even go right to sleep."

She laughed, for she knew what he meant. The sense
of urgency, of desperation, was gone; they had time, he
and she, time to discover and to build. "What are the
odds on that, do you think?" she asked, her eyes
twinkling as she took off her coat.

"I love it when you smile like that...perhaps sleep
could be delayed," he drawled.

As he hung up her coat, Liane knelt to pick up the
mail that had fallen on the carpet. A Visa bill and the
telephone bill, her monthly bank statement, a package
of free coupons, and a letter. She stared at the envelope,
a very expensive vellum envelope with her name and address printed in a precise, cramped hand that had not
changed in twenty years, and said in a voice from which
all the laughter had vanished, "This is from my father.
He never writes to me."

She was holding the letter in the very tips of her
fingers, staring at it as if it were a poisonous snake that
might lash out and bite her at any minute. Jake said,
"Open it and see what it says."

She stood up, reluctance in every move of her body.
"I could leave it until the morning."

Jake commented slowly, "You're really afraid of him,
aren't you—even now, eight years after you left home?"

She nodded, for it was useless to deny it. "I've always
been afraid of him."

"You're a grown woman who's made her own way in the world and is managing just fine—you don't need to be afraid of him."

In a flash of temper she retorted, "That's easy for you to say." If Jake hadn't knocked the pile of envelopes to the floor, she thought wretchedly, the letter would have stayed where it was until morning, and she and Jake would have been in her bedroom by now. "I'll read it tomorrow," she said.

"Read it now, Liane."

Although it was on the tip of her tongue to argue with him, she knew he was right. The letter had already come between them. Better to read it and be done with it. She tugged at the flap, extracted the single, closely written sheet of paper, and began to read.

A frown furrowed her forehead. She read the letter once, then again, striving to make sense of it, wishing the cold, sinking sensation in the pit of her stomach would go away. "I don't have a clue what he's talking about," she said finally. "He's saying how glad he is that I've accepted the money, and he wants me to get in touch with him to make the arrangements we agreed upon about Patrick." She looked over at Jake, anxiety and puzzlement warring in her face. "What money? What arrangements?"

Jake said with a careful lack of emotion that frightened her as much as the letter had, "May I see it?"

She passed it to him with patent unwillingness, her eyes glued to his face while he read it. He too was frowning; he looked every inch a policeman. "Have you taken money from him?" he rapped out.

"No—of course not. I don't understand what he means."

"He seems very sure that you have."

She said in a thin voice she scarcely recognized as her own, "Am I on trial again, Jake?"

He was looking over at the pile of mail on the table. "Wasn't there a bank statement in with those letters? Why don't you check it out?"

He didn't believe her. In a flood of primitive terror she cried, "Jake, I have not taken money from my father!"

"I'm not saying you have. But I'd like to get to the bottom of this—just see what the statement says."

Feeling as though she had been backed against a wall with a knife at her throat, Liane picked up the bulky envelope from the table. She did most of her business by check, and every month the checks were returned to her, along with a statement of credits and debits. Her fingers were cold, so cold she had trouble tearing the envelope open; but she had nothing to fear, she thought stoutly. She had not taken any money from her father. So the statement held no threat for her.

She put the pile of checks on the table and spread open the balance sheet. Then her throat closed with the same terror she had felt only moments ago. For the final balance, which should have been in the vicinity of a thousand dollars, was fifty-one thousand dollars.

She had never in her life had that much money.

Her eyes flew up the sheet. Nearly a week ago a deposit of fifty thousand dollars had been made into her account. With a trembling hand she pushed her hair back from her face, and wondered if this was really happening.

The hallway was as it had always been, and the table, when Liane reached out a hand to steady herself, had the same dent in its edge where Patrick had banged against it with one of his skates. And Jake was standing in front of her, indisputably real, although his face was a mask and his body had somehow withdrawn from her. She said numbly, "I didn't make that deposit."

He plucked the statement from her hand and scanned it rapidly. "A week ago," he said matter-of-factly. "Almost a week after I arrived here."

Clutching at straws, Liane said, "I have a bank card—someone else could have made the deposit."

"They'd have to know your code, and you're the only one to know that."

"There's an outside slot for deposits," she pointed out stubbornly. "To use that, all someone would have to know is my account number. Maybe Chester snooped in my handbag at the school."

"Maybe," said Jake.

"You don't believe me, do you?"

He replied heavily, "It's the scenario Chester outlined. The daughter holding out for money before she lets her father see his grandson."

The pain that ripped through Liane had nothing to do with her father and everything to do with Jake. Liane said, the words falling like shards of broken glass, "And now the money's arrived."

"It sure would explain why we haven't seen hide nor hair of Chester. Or why the kidnapping scheme that you were apparently so afraid of hasn't materialized."

"Apparently?" Liane repeated in a dead voice, wondering how one word could destroy so much.

When Jake suddenly hit the statement with his fingertips, the paper snapped with a crack like a gunshot. "The money's here!" he thundered. "That's a fact. Your father has given you fifty thousand dollars and now expects to see his grandson—that's also a fact. I deal in facts, Liane."

"Yes, you do, don't you?" she blazed. "That's all you know, Jake. You're drowning in facts, smothered in facts, buried alive in them! And you've lost touch with everything else. Real emotion. Sharing and trust and——"

"Facts don't lie!"

"But women do," she stated with immense bitterness. "Don't you think I'd have held out for more than a paltry fifty thousand? My father, like yours, is a very rich man."

"Fifty thousand must seem like a lot to you right now." He raked his fingers through his hair. "I can't read your mind so how should I know?"

Abruptly Liane was swamped by a fatigue so deep as to seem like death. She sagged against the wall, her face as white as the papers Jake was still clutching, and said tonelessly, "If you believe me capable of taking money from my father, of using Patrick as a pawn, then we're finished, you and I. It's over. Over almost before it's begun."

"We never should have started."

The words were a death knell. Far beyond tears, and certainly beyond pleading, Liane watched Jake put the letter and the statement back on the table on top of the envelope of free coupons. Nothing's free, she thought distantly. You pay for everything—and knew that at some time in the future she would pay for the happiness she had felt this evening in a pain beyond anything she had ever known. Dimly grateful for the anesthesia that at present seemed to be keeping that pain at bay, she heard Jake say, "I'll pack up my stuff and get out of here."

Turning on his heel, he went into the living room, and a few moments later Liane heard the slide of the zip on his suitcase and the small sounds of clothing being stuffed into a bag. It was better that he go. She could not bear for him to spend the night in her house when they were so deeply estranged from each other.

In a few minutes he came back into the hall, carrying his suitcase and his leather jacket. Liane said in a brittle voice, "What shall I tell Patrick?"

"I'll come back for a few minutes after school tomorrow to say goodbye to him."

"I'm working at the library tomorrow, so he'll be going to Megan's until six."

"Then I'll go to Megan's."

The words, she knew, were a cover for all that she and Jake were not saying. His eyes impaled her to the wall, eyes that were a turmoil of suppressed emotion. The silence between them seemed to scream in her ears; her heart was slamming against her ribs, her breathing so shallow that she felt light-headed. It seemed a strange combination of physical symptoms to usher in a broken heart, she thought, and wished he would go so that she could be alone.

"Anything I can think of saying sounds stupid and banal," Jake muttered. "I won't see you tomorrow... so I'll say goodbye now."

"Why say anything?" Liane asked, and, because that word goodbye had touched a nerve, flicking her with agony, her voice sounded cold and detached. "Just go."

He took a step toward her, as if he meant to touch her. Liane shrank back against the wall, knowing that if he did so she would begin to cry, and that she would die rather than cry in front of him. He halted immediately, his mouth a tight line. Then he said with a formality that to her ears sounded callous, "I hope that you can reconcile with your father, Liane. You don't need to be afraid of him—not now... and I'll try and make Patrick understand tomorrow why I have to leave. As for you, I—damn it, there aren't any words, are there? All I know is that I'll never forget you any more than I've ever understood you."

He did not say goodbye. He gave her a curt nod and crossed the hall in three swift strides. The door closed behind him, and seconds later she felt the draught of cold air against her legs. Then the engine of the wagon

roared into life. The tires crunched on the snow and the
engine retreated up the hill.

Her mind a blank, Liane checked the lock on the front
door and switched off the hall light. In the darkness the
walls slowly took form. Feeling her way, she went into
her bedroom, the room where she had known delight
beyond any imagining. She pulled her dress over her head
and got a clean nightgown out of the drawer—a
nightgown Jake had never seen. When she had put it
on, she decided that next she should brush her teeth.
However, as she rounded the end of the bed her bare
foot stubbed against a box lying on the floor, the box
in which she had so meticulously folded the length of
blue silk that Jake had bought in Thailand. As if she
couldn't help herself, she stooped, opened the box, and
ran her fingers over the slight roughness of the fabric,
hearing it rustle like the far-away sighing of wind in tall
trees. What had he said? "It was almost as though I
knew I'd meet you..."

With a tiny mewling sound of distress she ran into the
hall and up the stairs to Patrick's room, where she threw
herself across his bed, her nails digging into the spread.
She couldn't sleep in her room tonight. She couldn't.

Because Jake had gone. And he would not be back.

At five-past six the next day Liane pulled up outside Fitz
and Megan's old farmhouse. There was no sign of Jake's
wagon. Not that she had expected there would be. Jake,
by now, would be on the ferry, glad no doubt that the
expanse of water was ever widening between him and
the woman he could not bring himself to trust.

She had got through the day by rigorously avoiding
even the thought of his name; she did not think she would
be allowed this luxury at Megan's. Mentally steeling
herself, she got out of the car. Trojan and Bouncer gam-

bolled up to meet her. Patting them halfheartedly, she headed for the house.

Megan and Fitz were sitting by themselves at the kitchen table. The air smelled pleasantly of roast chicken and apple pie, and the wood was crackling cheerfully in the stove. Liane said brightly, "Is Patrick ready to go?"

"The three of them are upstairs having their supper," Megan announced.

"What's going on between you and Jake?" Fitz asked bluntly.

Liane had been afraid of this. "I really don't want to talk about it," she said, and cursed herself for the telltale quiver in her voice.

"Pour each of us a glass of wine, Fitz," Megan ordered, "and I'll serve the dinner. Then we're going to get to the bottom of this. Quite apart from the fact that you look like a gray day in winter, Liane Daley, your son was extremely upset this afternoon. The big glasses, Fitz—we need them."

Liane said loudly, "I'm not——"

Fitz neatly divested her of her coat, and pushed her down into the nearest chair. "Yes, you are. No point in arguing with Megs when she uses that tone of voice. I learned that years ago."

His lips were smiling at her through the tangle of his beard; his eyes were as light as Jake's were dark. Liane said, "Just because you're my best friends doesn't mean you can push me around," and burst into tears.

Her storm of weeping was as short-lived as it was violent. When she surfaced, Fitz had put a large pottery goblet of wine within reach and Megan was proffering a box of tissues. Liane blew her nose, took a big gulp of wine and said defiantly, "Jake thinks I'm a liar and an extortioner. As you would have known had you asked him. Now can we talk about the weather? Or about anything else other than him?"

"I did ask him," Megan said. "And was told in no uncertain terms to mind my own business. I told him you were my business. Whereupon he suggested, more or less politely, that I ask you." She grinned at her husband. "Then Fitz got in the act and said that if Jake thought you were dishonest in any way it was time he retired from the police force and became a human being instead . . . oh, it was quite exciting for a while. Not that we got anywhere."

"He doesn't listen," said Liane.

"We noticed that. So what's the story?" Fitz demanded.

To her own surprise Liane began pouring out all the events of the last two weeks, the words tumbling from her tongue as though by hearing them herself she might gain understanding. When she finished with a summary of her father's letter and the disastrous evidence of the bank statement, Megan drew a fascinated breath. "The money has to have come from your father."

"It's a setup," Fitz said thoughtfully, tugging at his beard as he always did when perplexed. "And what it accomplished was to get Jake out of the house . . . you're still convinced your father means to kidnap Patrick?"

Liane nodded unhappily. "When he threatens to do something, he's a man of his word."

"Well, the coast's certainly clear now, isn't it? No policeman living on the premises, standing in his way."

His musings had a horrible logic; Liane gaped at him. Megan put in excitedly, "And who was the first one to plant the story in Jake's mind that you were out for money? Chester! It didn't work right away . . . Jake went and stayed with you anyway. So what do they do next? Deposit money in your account with a nice little explanatory letter from your father. And this time it works. Jake leaves, and you and Patrick are alone again." With a smug smile she added, "Maybe *we* should apply for the police force, Fitz."

"Jake sure hasn't been using his brains," her husband commented.

"Well, he's in love," Megan said dismissively, as though the two states were mutually exclusive.

"He's not!" Liane snapped.

Fitz's amber eyes and Megan's green ones swerved around to Liane's face. "Of course he is," said Megan.

"Not a doubt," Fitz corroborated.

More tears welled up in Liane's eyes and streamed down her face. "He hates me," she wailed.

"Dearest Liane," Megan said forcefully, "hate is the opposite side of love, and if I ever saw a man in the grip of strong emotion, and fighting it every step of the way, it was Jake. Fitz, you've got his phone number, haven't you? All we have to do is call him and tell him all this, and he'll come back, I know he will."

Liane sat up straight in her chair, her tears forgotten. "Oh, no," she said, "you're not going to do that—not a chance!"

"Why ever not?" Megan asked. "Look at you; you're a wreck. Of course you want him back."

"The only way I want him back is if he makes up his own mind to come back," Liane insisted, her chin jutting. "He's got to trust me. Anything else is useless." She gave Fitz an unfriendly look. "And how did you get his phone number? *I* don't have it."

"I insisted he leave it with me," Fitz said blandly.

Unexpectedly Liane chuckled. "I'd like to have heard that little interchange."

Fitz leaned forward. "Wouldn't it be better if I spoke to him, Liane? It would save you a lot of heartache."

"No."

Megan poured herself more wine, her red hair more than usually tangled. "You're very stubborn," she said, her tone not complimentary.

"He believed my *father*, Megan. My father, rather than me. Yet I'm supposed to get down on my knees and beg him to come back?"

Fitz replenished his own glass. "You're in love with him," he stated.

"Oh, yes. More fool me."

"Hmm...why don't we eat?" Fitz suggested. "Maybe your admirable dinner will change her mind, Megan."

"Don't badger me, Fitz," Liane retorted. "I'm not going to change my mind."

Nor did she accept the offer they made later that evening for her and Patrick to stay in the old farmhouse for the weekend. "Our theories about Chester are all very clever," said Fitz, "but, if they're true, then Patrick could be at risk again."

Liane had already thought of that. "I can't stay—you know that—the Forsters expect me to be in the house, and the only way I can leave on Monday is to have Percy's cousin come in to take my place. What I will do is accept the loan of one of the dogs each night, though."

So at nine o'clock she and Patrick drove home with Bouncer breathing heavily in the back seat. The dog's presence, she soon saw, had the very desirable side effect of cheering her son up. She agreed that Bouncer could sleep on the floor in Patrick's room, and was not at all surprised when she went upstairs an hour later to find both boy and dog sprawled fast asleep on the bed.

She had to sleep in her own room that night—no choice. She put the box of silk in the very back of her wardrobe, changed the sheets on the bed, and lay down, thinking determinedly about all the work she had to do in the greenhouse before she and Patrick went skiing for the week. She did sleep; and over the weekend, by working very hard at the library, in the greenhouse, and at home getting ready for their trip, she managed to keep the worst of her emotions at bay.

Fitz took Patrick to his hockey game, and Megan invited the two of them for dinner both nights; not for the first time, Liane gave thanks for her friends. Patrick never mentioned Jake's name, and when Liane tried to talk about him the little boy listened politely and changed the subject as soon as he could.

The day after Jake left, Liane wrote a check to her father for fifty thousand dollars, and sent it to him registered delivery. She did not get any response. There was no sign of Chester.

Liane enjoyed the week in the Laurentians far more than she had expected to. She was an ardent and daring skier who had passed along her enthusiasm to her son, and the days spent high on the slopes in the cold, crisp air were good for both of them. When she went to bed in the chalet set among the spruce trees she fell asleep instantly, and the daily physical exercise made her passionate longing for Jake less acute. She had color in her cheeks when she and Patrick got home, and Megan's heartfelt, "You look wonderful!" was, if not totally true, at least considerably more accurate than it would have been the week before.

When she actually entered the house again after being away for seven days, Liane was glad of Bouncer's antics and Patrick's chatter, for the memories of Jake hit her like a blow as soon as she stepped across the threshold. He had stood in that doorway, he had propped his feet on that chair, he had kissed her in the hall and made love to her in the bed in her room. His presence surrounded her, his absence mocked and flagellated her, and the week she had been gone might never have happened.

That night, after Patrick and Bouncer had gone t
bed, she hauled the box from the back corner of he
cupboard and pulled out the length of silk. Stripping o
her clothes, she wrapped it around her body and looke
at herself in the mirror, dispassionately observing th
vivid blue of her eyes, the pale gleam of her skin, an
the way the fabric clung to the curves of her body. Jus
so must Jake have seen her, she thought, and wondere
if she was a fool not to write to him at the address o
the corner of the box, or phone him at the number tha
Fitz had given her.

But Jake had not believed in her. He had not truste
her. So what was the point of getting in touch with him

CHAPTER ELEVEN

IANE cried herself to sleep that night for the first time
nce Jake had left. But the next Saturday, out of some
ubborn need to assert her independence, she went into
harlottetown with Patrick and bought a pattern and
read to make a caftan out of the length of silk, and
at night she cut it out.

Bouncer continued to spend his nights on Patrick's
ed, although the threat of Chester had receded for
iane; with the passage of each day she was more in-
ined to believe that she had exaggerated her fears, as
ake had so often suggested. Her father, who had never
een a patient man, would have acted long before now.
o when on Thursday, her day off from the library, she
ent to the school to pick Patrick up at three-thirty, she
as not particularly worried when he didn't appear right
way. He was probably trading his hockey cards, she
ought indulgently, waving at a couple of his team-
ates as they ran for the bus.

The first two buses pulled out of the yard. Clancy
ashed down the steps, his lunch box banging against
is knee, and slid across the new-fallen snow, yelling to
couple of his friends. Liane rolled down her window.
Clancy! Have you seen Patrick?''

Clancy skidded to a halt and jogged over to the car,
aring at her in bewilderment. ''You picked him up at
oon—for the dentist.''

Liane's smile faded from her lips. ''No, I didn't,'' she
aid blankly. ''Wasn't he in school this afternoon?''

"Nope. The teacher had a note about the dentist, an after lunch your car was outside on the street, and Patric left."

"*My* car? I've been home all day, Clancy."

Clancy's freckled forehead puckered in though "Well, it looked like your car—it was a Volkswage and kind of old." His face brightened. "He's probabl gone on the early bus. P'raps he's at my place."

Liane did not think he was. "I'll go and see the teache about the note," she said, keeping her voice level wit an effort. "Thanks, Clancy. I'll see you later."

Forcing herself to keep panic at bay, she walked acros the school yard and up the steps. As she swung open th door, the smell of the air reminded her sharply of anothe school, in a valley miles away; tightening her lips, sh almost ran down the hall. Patrick's teacher, an energeti brunette fresh out of university, rummaged through th wastepaper basket and came up with the note. "I didn think much of it," she said, worried. "We get notes lik that all the time—I hope I haven't done anything wrong.

The note asked for Patrick to be excused at twelv forty-five for a dental appointment, and was signe "Liane Daley." The handwriting was not hers or he father's. Liane replied quietly, feeling her veins turn t ice, "No, you did nothing wrong. Thank you."

She hurried out to her car and drove home. Patric was not in the house, nor did his regular bus halt at th top of the hill to let him out. She then drove to Megan' Her heart was throbbing like that of a terrified bird, an her eyes were wide in her face when she burst in the bac door. Megan was rolling out pastry, her fingers coate in flour. "Liane! What's——?"

"Is Patrick here?" Liane demanded, biting her lowe lip as she waited for the answer.

"No...should he be?"

Liane collapsed in the nearest chair. "I think my father's taken him," she said in a voice drained of emotion.

Abandoning her pie crust, Megan called Fitz, who came out of the studio wiping his hands. With a kind of nerveless precision Liane recited what had happened. "I'd stopped worrying," she said helplessly. "Oh, Megan, what have they done to him? How did they get him in the car? He wouldn't have gone willingly, I know he wouldn't. Maybe they hurt him...he'll be so frightened."

"We'd better call the police right away," Fitz rapped. "Your father won't get away with this."

"He'll take me to court for custody," Liane said, her terror-filled eyes a stark blue. "He'll prove I'm not a fit mother."

Fitz's expletive was not one she had ever heard him use before. "We'll stand up in court and contradict him. You think you haven't made an impression on the community in the last couple of years, Liane? You think people haven't noticed how you take Patrick to hockey twice a week, and skiing on his breaks, and camping in the summer? Your father might have money on his side, but he doesn't have truth."

Despite his green-checked shirt Fitz could have been a prophet of old, railing against corruption among the elders; Liane felt strength flow back into her limbs, and with it the beginnings of anger. "I've always been so afraid of him," she confessed. "Ever since I was little. When he'd yell and rant and roar, I used to hide in the broom cupboard so he couldn't find me... Twice I saw him hit my mother."

She shivered, remembering the frightened little girl cowering in the darkness of the cupboard, her father's rages as awesome as thunder and as unpredictable as lightning. "But that's a long time ago, isn't it?" she went on, more to herself than to Megan or Fitz. Sitting up straight in her chair, recognizing this simple act as symbolic of a far more significant shift, she heard her voice gather force. "He shouldn't have taken my son. That's a terrible thing to have done. I'm going to phone him right now and tell him I want Patrick back."

When Murray Hutchins came to the phone, his voice was fainter than Liane recalled, but insidiously all the old fear crept into her limbs when he spoke. "Ah, yes," he said, "I've been expecting you to get in touch. Patrick should be arriving from the airport shortly. I won't keep you from him totally—that would be foolish. But don't try and get him back, will you?"

She thought of what Fitz had said, and how Jake had urged her to outgrow the reactions of a much younger Liane, and she remembered her own anger of a few moments ago. "Of course I'll get him back," she said, her knuckles white where she was holding the receiver. "I'm his mother and he——"

"I understand that a man you met on the road spent several nights in your bed, my dear... not the kind of behavior to which a seven-year-old should be exposed. As I'm sure any court in the land would agree. Don't push me too far, Liane—I want Patrick and I'll fight for him."

Her knees were trembling. Despising herself for her weakness, Liane retorted, "And I'll fight back! You're not going to get away with this—kidnapping's a serious offense. I'll phone later to speak to Patrick." Without saying goodbye, she replaced the receiver, and noticed with icy detachment that her hands were trembling as well.

Fitz had been listening unashamedly. "Good for you! Now we'd better call the police——"

Megan interjected, "I've got a better idea—why don't we call Jake instead?"

"Megs, you're a genius," her husband said warmly.
"We wrote the number in the back of the book, didn't
we?"

"You are not to call Jake," Liane said through gritted
teeth.

"We'll start with him," Fitz insisted, interposing his
big body between her and the phone as he began to dial.
And Liane, standing to one side, could not have said if
she was praying for Jake to be out or praying for him
to pick up the phone.

"Jake?" Fitz boomed. "Fitz Donleavy here. Liane's
father kidnapped Patrick this afternoon. How can we
go about getting him back?"

There were five seconds of dead silence. Then Liane
heard the faint crackle of Jake's voice, punctuated by
grunts from Fitz. "Sounds good," Fitz said finally.
"Here she is."

He passed the receiver to Liane. "He wants to talk to
you."

Gingerly she took the receiver. "Hello," she mumbled,
and, her breathing suspended, waited to hear what he
would say.

"I'll get Patrick back for you," Jake said forcefully.
"You're not to worry, do you hear? You'll have him
back by nightfall."

The timbre of his voice cut through all her fears for
her son; it was as if Jake were standing in the room with
her, so close did he sound. She tried to think of a reply
that would make sense, failed utterly, and heard him
rap, "Liane—are you still there?"

"Yes," she whispered. "He'll be frightened...I'm so
afraid they'll have hurt him."

"If they have, they'll have me to answer to," he said
so savagely that Liane flinched. "Liane, please stop
worrying! Patrick knows me—he won't be afraid to leave
with me. I'll fly from here to Halifax, leaving in about

half an hour, and once I've got him we'll flip over to the island. He'll be home by bedtime—much as he might prefer it to be midnight."

Unable to laugh at this smallest of jokes, Liane knew she had to warn Jake of what he might expect to hear. "My father knows about you and me—that we had an affair. He's threatened to use that, Jake." It was the first time she had used his name; it sounded foreign on her tongue.

"He won't dare to, not with me," Jake said forbiddingly. "I'm more than a match for your father. You be at the airport by nine tonight, and Patrick and I will be there." Then his voice changed, softening so that she felt clothed in a powerful mingling of warmth and pain, and almost tangibly reminded of the strength of his arms around her. "Don't be frightened, Liane. I've fouled up just about everything in your life since I met you, but I swear I won't foul this one up. Get Fitz to drive you to Charlottetown, and I'll drive you home. Take care."

The receiver clicked in her ear and she was left with the steady hum of a broken connection. She put the phone back in its cradle, and heard his voice echo in her ears. "I've fouled up just about everything in your life..."

Fitz said with immense approval, "A man of action. Private jets and the whole works."

Liane gave him a blank look. "Private jets?"

"Didn't he tell you? His first cousin owns a fleet of corporate jets—Jake's going to commandeer one of them." Fitz chuckled. "He'll probably get to Halifax before Patrick does."

"Fitz, this isn't a laughing matter!"

Fitz's face fell much as Patrick's tended to when Liane chided him. Megan patted her husband on the arm. "Talking to Jake has upset her."

Talking to Jake had set every nerve in her body on edge, Liane thought miserably. "Sorry, Fitz," she said with a shamefaced smile. "Here I am being a grump at five in the afternoon."

Fitz gave her one of his bear hugs. "Time we got the wine out," he decided. "This love affair of yours is going to turn us all into alcoholics."

"Just as long as you're sober enough to drive me to the airport by nine."

Fitz's reply was unquestionably sincere. "I wouldn't miss it for anything."

Megan finished her pie, and set Liane to work making a salad, and within the hour they were all seated around the table eating. The meat pie was excellent. Liane discovered she was hungry, for talking to Jake had relieved some of the terrible burden of fear she had been carrying ever since she had read the note about the fake dental appointment. Jake was the best person to try and get Patrick back. She had no idea how he would do it, and perhaps that was just as well. But she would not want to be Chester right now. Or her father.

She chewed mechanically, focusing all the love she felt for Patrick in an unspoken message of encouragement and comfort. Jake's coming, Patrick...Jake will get you out of there. Patrick, she thought dryly, would probably be delighted to be rescued by Jake. But what would happen if, once they were home, Jake left them on the doorstep?

Megan touched her on the arm, smiling at her. "I've asked you twice if you'd like more salad."

"Oh, no, thanks...Patrick *will* be all right, won't he?"

"I have every faith in Jake," Megan replied, patting Liane's arm for emphasis.

Liane had faith in Jake the policeman; but her faith in Jake the man had been sorely tried. And which one would she be meeting in Charlottetown at nine o'clock tonight?

Fitz and Liane were standing in the arrivals area of the airport by eight-thirty. Liane had insisted they get there early, partly because once the dinner dishes were washed and put away she couldn't stand doing nothing, and partly because she couldn't bear the thought of not being there to greet Patrick if he should arrive early.

He was not early. Nine o'clock came, then five-past, ten-past, twenty-past—by which time Liane had left uncertainty behind and was in an agony of fear. Something had gone wrong. Jake had not been allowed entry to her father's house. He had been arrested for illegal entry. Patrick had been taken somewhere other than the big brick mansion near the sea. Jake had been hurt. Patrick was not fit to travel.

Around and around her brain went, frantic as an animal in a cage as it circled these same possibilities again and again, yet too frightened to encompass any worse scenarios. She looked at the big round clock face once again. Nine twenty-two. It had moved exactly two minutes since the last time she had looked.

"There they are!" Fitz exclaimed.

Liane whirled. "Where?" she said stupidly.

Then she saw them. Hand in hand, Jake and Patrick were coming through the sliding doors. Under the fluorescent lights Patrick looked pale, his eyes shadowed as they always were when he was tired. As soon as he saw his mother he dropped Jake's hand and ran toward her.

Liane ran as well, stooping as he catapulted into her arms, his weight almost knocking her backward. "Patrick!" she gasped. "Oh, darling, are you all right?"

He was holding her with a feverish strength that said more than words how glad he was to see her. She eased her head back, searching his face. There was a small bruise on his cheekbone and his hair was tousled, but no more than if he had been playing hockey. "Did they hurt you?" she asked. "Patrick, I've been so worried! I'm *so* glad you're safe."

"They put something over my face, just like the time I had the appendix operation," Patrick said, grimacing. "I didn't like that very much, 'cause I thought it was you in the car... then when I woke up I was at Gramps's house." He added with some satisfaction, "I threw up all over the carpet."

A man had walked up to them. Liane's eyes traveled the length of his body from his mountain boots and navy cords to his down-filled jacket, coming to rest on his face with its familiar dark eyes and black hair. "Jake," she said. One of the things she had worried about from eight-thirty to five to nine was what on earth she would find to say to him; now that he was in front of her the problem solved itself. She got to her feet, keeping her arms tightly wrapped around her son, and said simply, "I can't thank you enough for what you've done. To have Patrick safe..." Her eyes flooded with tears. She blinked them back, and added very naturally, "Shall we go home? We can talk on the way."

His smile was stiff. "I ordered a rental car. I just have to pick it up... hello, Fitz."

"Good work!" Fitz said, pumping Jake's hand as energetically as if it were the handle of the old water pump in the barn. "James Bond had better look to his laurels."

Jake gave a reluctant grin. "Hardly... I did very little, actually. Excuse me for a minute, will you?" And he strode off in the direction of the car-rental counters.

"Closemouthed so-and-so," Fitz commented. "You've got your work cut out for you, Liane." He hunkered down by the little boy. "Quite an adventure you've had. Clancy'll be waiting to hear every detail. You hungry?"

"We had something to eat on the plane. It's a private jet, Mom, you should see it—with a kitchen and a bar and two bathrooms, one with a shower, and I was in the cockpit with the pilot—he's a friend of Jake's. It was neat!"

"Neat" was Patrick's highest word of commendation. Liane smoothed his hair, again feeling the tightness in her throat and the surge of tears; the other worry, that she had so assiduously refused to consider as the hands of the clock had crept around its face, was that Patrick, like Daniel, might be dead.

She could admit it now that he was safely in her arms. And she could admit also that in the deep recesses of her mind she had feared for Jake's safety.

Through a mist of tears she saw Jake come striding toward them. His jacket was slung over a Scandinavian sweater patterned in grays and blues—casual clothes, with no obvious signs of a gun, yet she would not want to have him as her enemy. He said brusquely, dangling a set of keys in his hand, "No problem—the car's outside in the parking lot. Shall we go?"

The four of them went out into the cold, star-etched night. Fitz said heartily, "Come and see us, Jake—glad to have you any time. And I'll add my thanks to Liane's—a good job. I'll look forward to all the details. Including——" he ruffled Patrick's hair "—who cleaned up the carpet." He kissed Liane's cheek, and ambled off between the double row of cars, a giant of a man who did not look as though he had a creative bone in his body.

Jake stopped by a gleaming sedan. Wanting to break the silence, Liane remarked, "What a gorgeous car, Jake—it's huge."

Jake said gruffly, "Thought you and Patrick might want to sit together in the front."

There were three sets of seat belts across the front seat. Liane said, "That was sweet of you—dammit, why do I keep on wanting to cry?"

Patrick said, grinning up at her, "I cried a little bit, when I came to and didn't know what was happening."

At seven-going-on-eight he was not as ready to admit to tears as he had been at five. Liane smiled back and replied feelingly, "I bet you did."

Jake opened the door, Patrick sat between them, and they drove off. About to ask her son for all the details, Liane heard him ask, "When can we go and visit Gramps, Mom? A proper visit."

Her jaw dropped. She had been quite prepared for Patrick to hate his grandfather after the day's events. "You'd want to?" she asked, feeling her way.

"Yeah...he used to collect baseball cards when he was a kid and he said he'd show 'em to me."

"Yes, not 'yeah,'" Liane corrected automatically, thinking fast. "I didn't expect you to like him very much after what he did today, Patrick."

"After I got sick, it was okay—up till then I didn't feel so hot." Patrick snuggled into her pink jacket, the one she had been wearing the first time she had met Jake. "Mrs. Petrie gave me some ice cream, and then he sort of stood around looking at me, like he didn't know what to do next. So I told him all about my hockey team and how you take me to the games, and then he showed me his house. All those rooms just for him."

Mrs. Petrie was the housekeeper, a woman of fearsome efficiency, and the only person Liane had ever known who could order her father around. "What kind of ice cream?"

"Swiss chocolate almond," Patrick said with gusto. "I showed her how to add pop and make a float. That was after she cleaned the carpet. She said the float tasted

really good, but Gramps said champagne and strawberries were more to his liking.''

This was obviously a direct quote. Liane smothered a
smile; it sounded as though Patrick, in less than an hour,
had disrupted the routine of the brick house quite com-
mendably. She said cautiously, ''Did your grandfather
want you to visit?''

''After Jake came, and when me and Jake were ready
to leave, he said he'd be honored if I would come again
and bring my hockey card collection with me. You can
come too, Mom. He said so.'' Patrick paused, trying to
smother a yawn. ''You know old Mrs. Hatchett, who
lives up the road all by herself, and likes to have the
school kids go in for a visit? He reminded me of her.
Sort of lonesome.''

Of all the words Liane might have chosen to describe
her father, that would not have been one of them. She
said, even more cautiously, ''I expect we could go for a
visit, Patrick. Some time.''

''That's good,'' Patrick replied sleepily, his eyelids
beginning to droop. ''Can I go see Clancy tonight?''

''Tomorrow,'' his mother said.

The boy did not argue, for he had fallen asleep. Liane
pressed a kiss on the top of his head, her heart over-
flowing with gratitude for his safety.

She glanced over at Jake. He was staring straight ahead
at the road, his profile a series of angular lines that did
not encourage communication. She said prosaically,
''He's tired out.'' Jake nodded and flicked on his high
beams.

She couldn't be angry with Jake, not when she owed
him so much...could she? She added with rather
overdone politeness, ''Did you run into any trouble?''

''None whatsoever.'' A wintry smile crossed Jake's
face. ''The housekeeper was in the middle of scrubbing

what looked like a genuine Aubusson when I rang the front door. I suggested baking soda.''

"You don't mean to tell me they just let you walk in the door and then ten minutes later walk out with Patrick?"

"Well, no, it wasn't quite that simple. Chester, who does not improve upon acquaintance, was prepared to get nasty until I showed him the error of his ways. Then your father tried to throw his weight around—metaphorically speaking—so he and I had a little talk. Whereupon any urge he might have had to take you to court and blacken your name deserted him."

"Jake," said Liane in exasperation, "what did you *do*?"

"Nothing very subtle. Your father is a big fish in a small pond. Mine is a big fish in a big pond. Mine could ruin yours with two or three carefully placed phone calls—I just thought I should point that out to him."

"Oh," said Liane, adding naively, "Your father must be *very* rich."

"Very."

"So my father will never try to kidnap Patrick again?"

"Never."

"You don't look like the son of a very rich man," she commented, glancing over at his unpretentious clothes.

"I always wanted to make my own way in life. Not hang on to his coattails."

There was a dismissive note in Jake's voice. End of conversation, thought Liane, and said calmly, "That's right. You told me you left home at sixteen. So how do you get along with your father now that you're older?"

"For two men whose value systems are almost totally opposed, and who share a somewhat stormy past, we get along remarkably well," Jake said wryly. "As I would suspect Patrick and your father would get along, given half a chance."

Direct hit. "If my father's lonesome it's his own fault," Liane asserted hotly.

Jake glanced at her over Patrick's head; he had made very little eye contact since they had left the airport. "There's something I want you to do," he said.

"Oh?" Her tone was not encouraging.

"I want you to go and see your father. On your own. It's time you laid that particular ghost to rest."

"He's no ghost!"

Jake said patiently, "He's an elderly man who's lost a son and thereby lost his grip on the future. He did a great wrong to try and seize the future in the form of Patrick—I'm not excusing or condoning that. But if you went to see him—and I mean really *see* him, Liane—you'd find pitifully little to be afraid of. For Patrick's sake, if for no other reason, I'd like you to go."

She stared straight ahead at the black ribbon of road edged by dirty banks of snow. Refusing to commit herself, she answered, "Perhaps I will."

"Good. I'll stay with Patrick tomorrow, and I'll phone Miss what's-her-name at the library and tell her you were called away on urgent family business."

"Tomorrow?" Liane repeated, feeling her temper rise. "What do you mean, tomorrow?"

"The jet's at the airport so you can fly to Halifax—a car will be there for your use, and you can fly home all in the same day. Simple."

"How nice of you to arrange my life for me!"

"I will not try and arrange it in any other way, I swear," Jake said tightly. "Seriously, Liane, it's a good time for you to go, while your father's still feeling chastened and while Patrick's visit is fresh in his mind. And it won't cost you a cent."

Underlying anger at Jake's cavalier methods and trepidation at the thought of facing her father was another emotion: hope. If she went to Halifax tomorrow, Jake would still be here when she got back. And in all honesty she suspected Jake was right, that it was time she confronted her father as an adult and attempted to build a new relationship with him, however tenuous that might be. A relationship, moreover, that included Patrick.

"Very well," she said stiffly. "I'll go."

"Good. You should make a fairly early start...I'll give Joe—he's the pilot—a call tonight to arrange it."

Feeling as though she had been picked up by a whirlwind and set down in a place where everything had subtly shifted, Liane said nothing. A mile further on Jake took the side road to Hilldale, and then swung down the Forsters' driveway. The house was in darkness because she had never thought to turn on any lights when she had run through the rooms at four o'clock this afternoon calling for Patrick. It seemed a lifetime ago.

Jake turned off the engine. "I'll carry Patrick up to his room," he said, and unbuckled the boy's seat belt.

Liane climbed out of the car. Her limbs felt stiff and she was aware at some level of a deep emotional exhaustion. But she could not afford to give in to that, because somehow she had to break through Jake's reserve. She wanted him in her bed tonight, wanted his naked body next to hers, wanted to fall asleep beside him and wake up enfolded in his arms.

He had not touched her once since they had met at the airport.

He was gathering Patrick's limp body into his arms. She remembered how he and her son had walked hand in hand from the plane, and felt a pang of what could only be jealousy. Horrified with herself, she found her key and led the way into the hall, switching on the light. After Patrick had stumbled into the bathroom and stumbled out again, Jake carried him upstairs, Liane undressed him, and they both got him into bed. The room was dark and the task intimate; Liane felt her nerves stretch to the breaking point as she kissed her son good-night. She then walked downstairs, knowing that Patrick had fallen asleep again even before she had left the room, achingly aware of Jake following her.

In the hall she turned to face him, standing between him and the door, the overhead light shining on the vulnerable curve of her mouth and on her anxious blue eyes. The pink of her jacket emphasized the pallor of her face as she rested her hand on the sleeve of his sweater and said tentatively, "Jake?"

"Let me use your phone to call Joe, will you?"

She let her hand fall to her side. "You know where it is."

He went into the kitchen, and Liane heard the low murmur of his voice. Then she heard him dial a second number. She stayed where she was, huddling her jacket around her because she was cold and only Jake could warm her, and watched as he came back into the hall. He said, "The weather reports are good for the next twenty-four hours, so he'd like to leave by ten...that okay with you? It'll give you time to get Patrick off to school before you go."

She nodded, realizing she would have agreed to five in the morning or nine at night, for what difference did it make? "Fine," she said.

"Joe'll be waiting for you in the departures area—short guy, balding, in a blue uniform. He'll let you know how long you can be with your father, too—he wants to be back in Charlottetown by evening. And I let your father know you'd be coming."

"I'm not getting out of this, am I?" said Liane, wondering if she was being fanciful to think that Jake's eyes were like black pits, swallowing her in darkness.

He said harshly, "Well, I'd better be going. Have a safe journey tomorrow."

Her heart gave an uncomfortable jolt in her breast. "Going?" she repeated in a voice that seemed to come from a long way away. "Aren't you staying here?"

He shook his head. "No need . . . you'll be quite safe now."

"It wasn't my safety I was thinking of, Jake."

"I made arrangements this morning to stay in a motel near the airport."

His face gave nothing away, while his voice held as little emotion as if he were talking to a stranger and not to the woman he had made love to in the bed not twenty feet away. Liane told him doggedly, forgetting pride— for what did pride have to do with the way she felt about Jake? "I want you to stay here. Please, Jake." In magnificent understatement she added, "I've missed you."

Something flickered across his face, so rapidly that she might have imagined it. His eyes dropped as he did up the zip on his jacket, and he said with a cold formality far more devastating than anger, "Then you're a fool, Liane."

As he took the car keys out of his pocket, she stood her ground, sick at heart, his words thrumming dully in her tired brain. A fool, a fool, a fool . . . Then he elbowed past her, the contact shuddering through her body. She watched him go, her throat muscles paralyzed, her emotions a tangle of anger, pain and exhaustion. He closed the door with a decisive snap.

Like a figure captured by the snap of a camera, Liane stood still. She had told him what she wanted. But he had not heard her. Because, quite clearly, he did not want what she wanted.

CHAPTER TWELVE

AT ELEVEN-FIFTY the next morning Liane was ringing the doorbell of her father's house. The pines that flanked the long curve of the driveway were swaying in the wind that blew cold from the Atlantic and she heard the distant rattle of waves on the rocky shore. Mrs. Petrie opened the door, and nodded with more politeness than warmth. "Good morning, Miss Hutchins. We were expecting you."

Liane did not like being called Miss Hutchins. Sitting in the plush seat of the private jet as it winged across the strip of water between Prince Edward Island and Nova Scotia, she had decided that today was to be a day of changes. Jake was first on the list. When she got home tonight she would not meekly allow him to walk past her into the darkness as she had last night; she would fight for him, even if that meant telling him she loved him. And in her father's house, to the best of her ability, she was going to act from her strengths as a mother and a provider rather than from her weaknesses as a frightened, subservient daughter. On her last visit she had run from her father's anger. She was not going to run from him today.

So she said, handing over her pink jacket with a pleasant smile, "I use my mother's maiden name now, Mrs. Petrie—Daley." Bending to change from her boots to her best shoes, she added, "I do hope the carpet has recovered from my son's visit yesterday."

"A most unfortunate accident," said Mrs. Petrie. "However, there should be no lasting damage. Mr. Brande was very helpful."

Liane's smile did not waver. "An accident that was scarcely Patrick's fault."

Mrs. Petrie inclined her head, for if she was a cold woman she was also a fair one. "That is certainly true," she agreed. "Mr. Hutchins is in the drawing room."

Liane straightened her spine, kept her smile firmly in place, and opened the tall paneled door into the drawing room. "Good morning, Father," she said.

Her father put down the magazine he had been reading, and got to his feet. "Liane," he said. "Would you like coffee after your journey?"

She walked across the room, her heels tapping on the inlaid oak floor, and kissed him on the cheek, noticing with a touch of amusement that she had taken him by surprise. "No, thanks, I had some on the plane." She sank gracefully into a velvet wing chair. "I gather you enjoyed Patrick's visit yesterday?"

Murray Hutchins sat down opposite her, wincing a little as he crossed his legs. She added quickly, "Is your arthritis bothering you?"

"This confounded winter weather," he replied.

He looked shrunk in the big wing chair, wizened like a gnome. "You should be heading south and lying in the sun."

"I'm a busy man, Liane."

She ignored this undoubted red herring, and said with gentle persistence, "You didn't answer my question."

Her father frowned at her from beneath bushy white brows. "He's a young man who believes in speaking his mind."

"Thank you," she said serenely. "I've brought him up that way."

"Children were seen and not heard in my day."

"Which is perhaps why your emotions are still locked away inside you. To the detriment of all of us."

In his wrinkled face his eyes were still as blue as hers; they did not falter. "Let me offer you a sherry," he said.

"That would be lovely."

She watched as he tottered across the room, and did not offer to help when he had difficulty wresting the stopper from the crystal decanter. Had he always been so unsteady? Or had she never, as Jake had suggested, really seen him clearly before?

She did not want to think about Jake—not now when she needed all her wits about her. She took the glass from the ornate silver tray and sipped the pale, dry liquid. "Despite his outspokenness, would you like to see Patrick again?"

"I would not have expected such an offer after yesterday."

"Jake said that what happened yesterday will never happen again."

"It will not."

He took a gulp of sherry; he had never been a moderate man. Liane asked evenly, "Are you sorry for what you did?"

His blue eyes bored into hers. "You want your pound of flesh, don't you?" he said unpleasantly.

Inwardly Liane quailed, as she had always quailed before her father's anger. Outwardly she remained composed, her fingers curved a little too tightly around the stem of her glass, and made no reply.

Impatiently Murray Hutchins admitted, "I shouldn't have done it. It was wrong of me. Does that satisfy you?"

She nodded, for she knew that for him these were massive admissions. "I've done wrong, too," she said steadily. "I've been afraid of you for as long as I can remember, so I've kept Patrick from——"

"You don't look afraid of me right now!"

He was glaring at her. "I'm not, actually," Liane said, unable to repress her smile. "A lot of things have changed since I saw you last. I'd be happy to see you more often, and to bring Patrick with me—he'd like to visit you, too."

The glass in her father's gnarled hand shook so badly that the sherry slopped almost to the rim. "How do you know?"

"He said so."

A pleased smile passed like the winter sun over her father's face, and was as quickly extinguished. "He only wants to get his hands on my baseball cards," he growled.

"He liked you, Dad," insisted Liane, who in all her twenty-seven years had only rarely used this diminutive.

"Gramps. Dad. What's the world coming to?" Murray grumbled. "Are you sure he liked me?"

Liane laughed, a delightful laugh of genuine amusement. "Come on, tell the truth, you're dying to see your grandson again."

"I wouldn't mind seeing him again, no."

"You're a hypocrite," Liane said amiably. "Aren't you going to offer me another glass of that admirable sherry?"

"Aren't you afraid I'll try and influence your son to take over my business? Because I will, Liane."

She said, choosing her words with care, "Patrick is only seven, but he already has fairly definite ideas on what he wants and does not want. At the moment he wants to play hockey and build a rocket to the moon, and he doesn't want to study English. I think you'll find him more than a match for you, Dad. And, who knows, maybe when he's older he will want to take over the business? But only because he wants to, not because you've brainwashed him."

Murray frowned at her. "You're being very forth-right."

"Yes," Liane said in faint surprise, for it had been a great deal easier than she had anticipated, "I am."

"So when will you bring him?"

"I'll check my schedule when I get home, and my first free weekend we'll come over—within the next three weeks, I promise."

He pushed himself out of the chair and took her glass, crossing the glowing crimson patterns of the antique Persian rug on his way to the decanter. His back to her as he poured more sherry into her glass, he said gruffly, "Thank you."

He had not actually said he was sorry for kidnapping and for his threats, and he had not been able to look her in the face when he thanked her. But to Liane these were minor concerns. She knew each had traveled a long way today—she probably further than her father; and she was more than content with all she had accomplished.

When Liane got home at seven-thirty that evening, Jake's rented car was nowhere to be seen. She let herself in the front door, knowing instantly that the house was empty, and saw a plain white envelope propped on the hall table, her name printed on it in blue ink. She ripped the envelope open and scanned the single sheet of paper it contained.

"Liane," it said. "I hope my returning Patrick to you has in some small way ameliorated my appalling lack of trust in you. Jake." Beneath this he had scrawled as an afterthought, "Patrick is at Megan's."

She turned the paper over, but that was all it said. Not "Dear Liane." Not "Love, Jake." Nor had he said that she would also find him at Megan's. She ran to the phone and dialed their number. Fitz answered. Forgetting to say who it was, she gasped, "Fitz, is Jake there?"

"Is that you, Liane? No, he insisted on leaving for the airport half an hour ago. Said he wanted to fly back to Ottawa tonight."

She and Jake must have passed on the road, Liane thought sickly. In the darkness she would not have seen him. And by now the jet would have taken off for the thousand-mile flight west. She sagged against the wall, all she had achieved that day like dust in her mouth. What good was her decision to make changes in her life if Jake wasn't here? Two people were needed for a relationship to change.

But Jake was gone. He had not waited to see her.

"Liane...you still there?"

"Yes," she whispered, "I'm here."

"I'll run Patrick over. Be there in ten minutes."

She did not want to see Fitz. She wanted to see Jake.

All her movements automatic, Liane hung up her coat and pulled off her boots. She then went into the bathroom and repaired her makeup, trying to restore some color to her face. When the doorbell rang, she plastered a smile on her pink lips and opened the door.

"Hi, Mom," Patrick crowed, waving a sheet of paper at her. "Look at this!"

It was an English quiz on which he had made the unprecedented mark of seventy-one. Her smile far more genuine, she congratulated him, listened to all the various events of his day, and told him about the proposed visit to his grandfather. While Fitz made himself a cup of tea, she put Patrick to bed and read two more chapters of his latest science fiction book. Then she went downstairs to face Fitz.

Fitz, a man of the moment, had fallen asleep on the couch. Liane shook him awake. He yawned, grinned at her through the tangle of his beard, and said, "Megs and I think you should head for Ottawa as soon as you can pack your bags."

"Why?" asked Liane militantly. "So Jake can slam the door in my face?"

"So you can talk some sense——"

"He won't listen!"

"Neither will you."

Abruptly she sat down in the nearest chair. "I'm tired, Fitz, and not in the mood for an argument."

"No argument. Jake's a proud and reticent man who knows darn well how greatly he's misjudged you and who cannot get it through his thick skull that just possibly you might forgive him. It's up to you to convince him you do. You do, don't you?"

"So are you suggesting I leave for Ottawa right now?" she said sarcastically. "Hot on his tail?"

"You could wait until tomorrow. It's the weekend— no school, Megan and I will take Patrick, and I'll keep an eye on the house for you." He gave his moustache a triumphant swirl.

Liane suddenly dropped all pretense, her face mirroring her misgivings. "I'm scared to go, Fitz. I'm so vulnerable to him, and if he sent me away again I'm not sure I could bear it."

Fitz scowled mightily. "I'm almost sure he won't. But I guess there is that risk."

Risk. The word she had tossed around so blithely so short a time ago. Had she not sworn she would never take another risk? Liane bowed her head, gazing at her linked hands in her lap, thinking of all that Jake had given her and of all that he had taken away. "I will go," she said in a low voice. "Tomorrow, if I can get a flight."

She felt nothing. No surge of joy that she would see Jake again, no rush of hope, no flutter of panic. Just a strange, dead sense of waiting.

For the rest would depend on Jake.

* * *

The next morning a light snow was falling as Liane left for the airport. When she had made her bookings the night before, the only seats she could get were via Halifax and Montreal with a scheduled arrival in Ottawa mid-afternoon; she had put the ticket on her Visa. It was now up to its limit, because she had also used it on the ski trip to the Laurentians, and the spending money in her wallet had left just enough in her account to cover her bills. I'm going for broke, she thought, glancing at the lead gray sky as she took the main highway into Charlottetown.

The snowfall was heavier by the time she left her car in the parking lot. But the first leg of her flight took place without mishap, although the runways and the terminal building of the Halifax airport were blurred by whirling flakes of snow.

She had an hour's wait in Halifax. Trying to ignore how many flights were delayed or canceled, particularly those from the west, Liane had a coffee in the cafeteria and wandered around the gift shops. Although her flight was delayed twice, eventually it lifted off.

It was a bumpy flight. Ten minutes out of Dorval the pilot cautioned that they might have to backtrack to Moncton in New Brunswick because of the weather situation. But then, after a further delay, he made an impeccable landing under what must have been very difficult conditions. Montreal was a great deal closer to Ottawa than Moncton; Liane smiled to herself as they taxied to the gate.

A second announcement wiped the smile from her face. The flight was terminating in Dorval, the pilot advised in a soothing voice, due to the snowfall warning and increasing winds. The ongoing passengers would be put up in a nearby hotel and informed as soon as possible of the continuation of their flight. He then thanked them for their patience and cooperation.

Liane, feeling neither patient nor cooperative, filed out of the cabin and was herded into a bus. Now that she was on the ground she was amazed the pilot had been able to land at all. When she got to the hotel she'd find out about taking the train to Ottawa, she decided. She'd rather be at ground level in this.

However, the trains and the buses were all canceled, the word blizzard bandied about frequently and with varying degrees of excitability. She was stuck. She would have to make the best of it. At least the hotel and her meals were paid for by the airline, she thought, fingering the rather scanty stock of bills in her wallet, and using one of them to buy herself a paperback in the hotel lobby.

The time dragged past. Liane went to bed early, woke up to find that it was still snowing, and was told by the airline that no flights were scheduled until afternoon at the earliest. She could walk to Ottawa faster, she thought glumly, heading for the coffee shop, where she ate far too much breakfast.

By two in the afternoon the snow had all but stopped, the wind had died and the runways had been plowed. The backlog of aircraft was gradually cleared; at five-past four Liane's flight took off for Ottawa. She took a cab from the airport to Jake's address, a slow trip because of the number of snowplows and heavy-duty trucks on the streets, and paid the cabbie with two more of her precious bills. She stood on the pavement in her leather boots and her pink jacket, looking at his house.

It was a two-story brick and stucco dwelling set back from the street in a large garden with, she noticed professionally, some beautiful trees. He was renting it, he had told her once, with an option to buy when his career plans were more settled. She walked up the path, which had recently been shoveled, and rang the doorbell. She felt very nervous.

No one came to open the door. There was, she realized with a sinking heart, no red wagon parked in the driveway, which had also been shoveled. She rang the bell again, and, when there was no response, knocked loudly in case the bell was broken. Even if Jake was out, hadn't he mentioned a housekeeper?

Neither Jake nor the housekeeper answered the door. She walked around the side of the house, where a wooden gate led into the back garden past the garage; when she peered into the garage window she saw that it was, except for some garden equipment, empty. No sign of the red wagon. So Jake had to be out.

There was an attractive wooden bench inside the gate, shielded by some evergreens. Liane swiped most of the snow off it and sat down to think.

She had no idea where Jake was, although the shoveling that had been done made her think he would not be long. She counted her money, wondering if she had enough to take another cab into town and stay in a hotel overnight. She rather doubted that she had, unless the hotel was so cheap that she probably wouldn't want to stay in it anyway. She could always sleep on a bench at the airport, she thought sturdily. And she didn't really need any dinner.

Having decided to wait for a couple of hours, she settled herself more comfortably on the bench. Luckily it was not very cold, and the garden was sheltered from the wind. If Jake were not home by nine o'clock, she would go back to the airport and start phoning his number at regular intervals.

She should have told him she was coming. But she had been afraid that he would refuse outright to see her. Turning up on his doorstep had seemed a far better idea.

She read for a while until the light got too bad to see the words on the page. She walked up and down, stamping her feet to warm them, wishing she had worn her less glamorous but much warmer fleece boots. Resolutely she kept her mind away from the subject of food. And still Jake did not return.

Liane had slept very little the last three nights, and she had lived with tension ever since Patrick's kidnapping; eventually she put her small shoulder bag at one end of the bench, and lay down, pulling her black skirt down over her knees as far as she could. Telling herself she would stay only another thirty minutes, knowing she would never fall asleep because she was too hungry and her feet were too cold, she closed her eyes.

"For God's sake—*Liane*?"

She was beneath a frozen sea, walking through ice caverns that shone pale turquoise, translucent, unearthly. Her leather boots kept slipping on the ice, and her feet were cold...

Someone shook her hard by the shoulder. "Liane, wake up!" a loud voice said in her ear.

With an incoherent exclamation Liane sat bolt upright, her eyes wide open, and for a horrible moment she had no idea where she was. Then she focused on Jake's face, only inches from hers, felt the unyielding boards of the bench beneath her, and knew exactly where she was. "You came home," she said.

"You could have frozen to death," he said harshly. "If you hadn't left the gate ajar, I wouldn't have known you were here."

He did not look pleased to see her. Rather, he looked extremely angry. Liane was so cold she scarcely cared. She let her feet fall to the ground, and gave an involuntary cry of pain at the cramps in her knees. "For God's *sake*!" Jake exclaimed again, scooped her up in his arms, and tramped through the snow to the front door.

"Put me down," Liane ordered.

"And have you fall flat on your face on the path? Don't be silly!"

He shoved the door open with his foot, and strode inside, hitting it shut with his elbow. As the warmth of the house enveloped her, Liane realized she was shivering all over, and was quite unable to stop, even her teeth chattering like a distant rattle of snare drums. Jake said, kicking off his boots, "How long have you been outside?"

"Since about six."

"Do you know what the time is? Ten-thirty! You're damn lucky I came home as early as I did."

She sputtered incoherently, "The way you look I don't think I'm particularly lucky. What was her name?"

He stopped dead at the bottom of the stairs. "Pete," he retorted. "Peter Bennett—my cousin who owns the fleet of jets."

Pushing her hands under his jacket to find the warmth of his body, Liane said, "Pete's a nice name."

Shivering as she was, she could still feel the tension gripping Jake's body. He said hoarsely, not looking at her, "You're the last person I would have expected to find on my doorstep—what the hell are you doing here?"

Risk. Go for broke. "I'm here b-because I love you," Liane stuttered.

Unconsciously his arms tightened their hold. "I don't believe you. For God's sake don't play games—I can't stand it!"

"I d-do love you," she wailed. "Oh, Jake, I'm so cold!"

He stood still. "How can you possibly love me?" he flared. "When the chips were down I believed your father's version of events, not yours. I couldn't bring myself to trust you—because you're a woman."

She scanned his features one by one. He needed a shave and his eye sockets were dark-circled, sunk into his skull. "You look terrible," she said.

"Don't change the subject!"

"Look at me, Jake." With patent reluctance he dragged his gaze down to hers. His eyes were bloodshot. "What *have* you been doing to yourself?"

"Getting drunk," he replied economically. "At Pete's."

He did not smell of liquor. "Tonight?"

"Last night." He put her down so suddenly that she staggered. "Liane, you can't love me! I believed your *father*—not you."

"I know you did." She fought to control the tremors in her limbs, knowing she was battling for her life here. Her life and Jake's. "You've had lousy role models as far as women are concerned," she said. "Your mother, your father's mistresses, your wife—every one of them upped and left you."

"You're making excuses for me."

"I'm trying to understand!"

He gripped her shoulders so hard that she could feel the dig of his fingers through her jacket. "Are you saying that you forgive me?"

Fitz had used the word forgiveness; once again Fitz had known what he was talking about. "Yes," Liane said, wriggling her cold toes inside her boots and watching incredulity and hope war in Jake's eyes. "I forgive you. Why else would I be here?"

He said in a cracked voice, "I love you, too."

She had traveled hundreds of miles to hear those words. Yet now that he had said them she felt nothing. Her knees shaking so hard she would have given all the remaining money in her wallet for some of Megan's cranberry wine, far beyond saying anything but the truth, Liane croaked, "It's funny...you don't know how often

I've longed to hear you say those words. But now that you have, I—I'm not sure I believe you. Maybe the only reason you're saying them is because I've forced my way into your house and you're just being polite . . . I should never have come."

"Polite?" Jake repeated with an unamused bark of laughter. "Politeness has absolutely nothing to do with the way I'm feeling right now." His eyes raked her face, seeing the tension and vulnerability in the curve of her mouth. "I've loved you since that first moment you appeared out of a snowstorm in the middle of the Wentworth Valley."

"You have a funny way of showing it."

He said violently, "I didn't want to fall in love with you. I didn't want to fall in love with anyone."

She thrust her hands deep in her pockets. "Why did you get drunk last night, Jake?"

"Because I couldn't bear the emptiness of my house. Because I missed you so much I thought I'd die for want of you. Because I knew I'd thrown away something utterly precious. Shattered it beyond repair." His voice was corrosive with self-contempt. "And all because I was afraid to trust you."

Aching to smooth the pain from his face, she said, "I hate to hear you talk that way."

"Halfway through the bottle of rum, I poured out the whole sorry story to Pete. He told me I didn't deserve you, and that he had a jet going from Ottawa to Halifax this afternoon that could make a detour to Charlottetown, and that I'd damn well better get on it."

For the first time since she had arrived, Liane smiled. "Another Fitz."

"But it snowed all day and the jet was stuck in Toronto. Plus I've got one hell of a hangover." Jake gave her a crooked smile. "So the trip was delayed until tomorrow morning."

"But *you* were coming to see *me*?"

"Yeah. I was ninety-nine per cent sure you'd shov me the door. But I had to try." His eyes, full of strain met hers. "Because—and I don't blame you for not be lieving me—I do love you. More than I can say."

Liane's body gave a sudden uncontrollable shudder "I'm starting to believe you. I think."

In sudden concern he said, "You're cold. And yo look worn out." He hesitated. "Will you stay here to night? You can sleep in the spare room if——"

"Don't you want to sleep with me any more?"

"Of course I do!"

The intensity with which he spoke made Liane's hear beat faster. "That's good," she said. "Because I don' want to sleep in the spare room, and I can't afford t go anywhere else. I don't normally park myself on garde benches in the aftermath of a blizzard."

"Do you mean to tell me you don't have any money?" Picking her up again, Jake started to climb the stairs From the corner of her eye she saw pen and ink drawing on William Morris wallpaper, and heard the mellifluou chiming of a grandfather clock.

"Forty-three dollars."

"Did you have an alternative plan other than freezin, to death on my bench?"

"Sleep at the airport. It's free."

He said, pushing the bathroom door open, "You mus love me. Explanations later, Liane. I'll start the wate and get you something warm to wear...are you hungry?"

Jake was looking more like himself, and less like man tormented by all the demons in hell. She grinne at him through her lashes. Her teeth were no longer jit tering against each other—a distinct improvement—an Jake had twice said that he loved her. "I ate an ope sandwich in Montreal at noon. Courtesy of the airline."

"I've got some soup in the freezer—I'll heat it up."

As he passed her a thick wool robe through the door, she added saucily, "If we're going to spend the night together, I insist you shave."

"Giving orders already, huh?" The laughter faded from his face. He said quietly, "I love you so much, Liane. With all my being, I love you."

Shaken to her soul, Liane felt tears spill from her lashes. "I love you, too," she whispered, and knew the simple words for a vow.

"Then we'll be all right, won't we?" He gave her a smile of immense tenderness. "Take your time. I'll be downstairs."

Her reflection in the mirror was that of a woman who had been given a gift beautiful beyond belief. Liane bent and turned on the hot tap.

She soaked in the tub, used Jake's Calvin Klein powder liberally all over her body, and wrapped the deep green folds of the robe around her. Then she went downstairs, finding her way to the kitchen, an ultramodern room adorned with every conceivable appliance. Following her fascinated gaze, Jake said, "I like gadgets—half the fun of cooking. Here, sit down... are you warmer?"

"Much." Suddenly shy, aware that under the robe she was naked, Liane bent her attention to the bowl of excellent leek and potato soup and the thick slabs of crusty French bread. Several minutes later she gave a sigh of repletion. "That was wonderful. You saved my life."

"Any time. So when did you leave the island, Liane?"

Briefly she ran through the vicissitudes of her journey, finishing with the bench. "I never thought I'd go to sleep."

"Snowstorms seem to follow us around, don't they? Why didn't you phone and let me know you were coming?"

"I thought you'd tell me not to. Would you have, Jake?"

"Friday night I probably would have... I was to
ashamed of the way I'd behaved to be anywhere nea
you. I'd belittled your fear that Patrick might be kid
napped, I'd accused you of trying to get money out o
your father, I'd aligned you with all those women who'
been with my father... and on each count I was wrong."

Like a man mesmerized, he took her hand in his an
smoothed the slender length of her fingers. "Your fathe
did kidnap Patrick, you're absolutely honest abou
money, and you're brave and responsible and loving.
couldn't have constructed a more false picture of you—
how could I ever make amends for that?"

"So you hightailed it back to Ottawa as fast as yo
could," she said, wondering how much longer she woul
have to wait before he kissed her.

He grimaced. "I figured you must despise me. Bette
to get out of your life and out of Patrick's, too. Becaus
apart from falling in love with you, I was also gettin
far too attached to him. So yeah—I ran away."

"But on Saturday—thanks to Peter and the rum—
you changed your mind?"

"By Saturday night I knew I'd never have a moment'
peace if I didn't at least try to repair some of the damag
I'd done. I'll never distrust you like that again, Liane
I swear I won't." Laughter suddenly flashed across hi
face. "I'm not saying we won't fight sometimes—I'd b
very surprised if we don't. But I promise I won't dump
all my past on those fights."

"I can promise the same thing, Jake... because th
visit with my father went really well." She went on t
describe it, and also told him about Patrick's quite as
tonishing mark in English. And then she ran out of thing
to say.

There was a short, charged silence. Jake said softly
"Come to bed with me, Liane? Or shall I propose in th
kitchen first?"

She blushed. "I've been wanting to go to bed with you for the last seventy-two hours. And you can propose anywhere and any time you like."

"Marry me," Jake said, his dark eyes caressing her face. "Please marry me."

"Oh, yes," Liane agreed, her features radiant with happiness. "I'll marry you. For my sake I'll marry you because I love you, and for Patrick's sake I'll welcome you as his father. Just as I'm sure he will."

For a moment Jake's face clouded. "My job's probably going to be here in Ottawa—you'd have to move away from Megan and Fitz, and Patrick would have to leave all his friends."

"He'd be gaining a father, though. And, although I'd miss Megan and Fitz, I'm sure we'd visit back and forth." She smiled at him. "Could we live in the country?"

"Of course we could. We'll buy a farm near a hockey rink."

She said, knowing she had to give voice to the words, "I understand that Patrick will never take your son's place. But I also know you will love Patrick as if he were your own son."

Jake cleared his throat, a look on his face that she had never seen before. He said huskily, "I will—I promise."

She stood up by her chair, wanting him so badly that her whole body ached with primitive hunger. "You did mention bed, didn't you?" she asked.

"It's been as much as I can do to keep my hands off you ever since I found you on the bench."

Liane guided his palm to the swell of her breast under his robe. "And now you don't have to."

For a moment he held back. "You do believe I love you?"

Her answer was instinctive; she walked into his arms, drew his head down, and kissed him full on the mouth. "Yes," she whispered. "I believe you."

He said exultantly, "I feel as though I've been let out of prison to be able to say those words to you, and to see the light in your eyes when I do." Drawing the lapels of the heavy robe apart, he drank in the ivory perfection of her body. "We'd better go upstairs. Or we'll be making love on the kitchen floor." Then, lifting one hand to smooth the hair back from her face, he added, "You've had a rough three days—you're sure you're not too tired?"

Mischief danced in her eyes. "I'm tired, yes. But I'm sure you can convince me to make love to you, Jake."

Nor was it at all difficult for him to do so.

HARLEQUIN PRESENTS®

A Year DOWN UNDER

In 1993, Harlequin Presents celebrates the land down
under. In June, let us take you to the Australian Outback,
in OUTBACK MAN by Miranda Lee,
Harlequin Presents #1562.

Surviving a plane crash in the Australian Outback is
surely enough trauma to endure. So why does Adrianna
have to be rescued by Bryce McLean, a man so gorgeous
that he turns all her cherished beliefs upside-down? But
the desert proves to be an intimate and seductive setting
and suddenly Adrianna's only realities are the red-hot
dust *and* Bryce....

Share the adventure—and the romance—
of A Year Down Under!

Available this month in
A YEAR DOWN UNDER

SECRET ADMIRER
by Susan Napier
Harlequin Presents #1554
Wherever Harlequin books are sold.

Where do you find hot Texas nights, smooth Texas charm,
and dangerously sexy cowboys?

WHITE LIGHTNING

by Sharon Brondos

Back a winner—Texas style!

Lynn McKinney knows Lightning is a winner and she is
totally committed to his training, despite her feud with her
investors. All she needs is time to prove she's right. But
once business partner Dr. Sam Townsend arrives on the
scene, Lynn realizes time is about to run out!

CRYSTAL CREEK reverberates with the exciting rhythm of
Texas. Each story features the rugged individuals who live
and love in the Lone Star State. And each one ends with
the same invitation...

Y'ALL COME BACK...REAL SOON!

**Don't miss WHITE LIGHTNING by Sharon Brondos.
Available in June wherever Harlequin books are sold.**

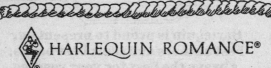 

Harlequin is proud to present our best authors and their best books. Always the best for your reading pleasure!

Throughout 1993, Harlequin will bring you exciting books by some of the top names in contemporary romance!

In June,
look for
*Threats and
Promises* by

BARBARA
DELINSKY

The plan was to make her nervous....

Lauren Stevens was so preoccupied with her new looks and her new business that she really didn't notice a pattern to the peculiar "little incidents"—incidents that could eventually take her life. However, she did notice the sudden appearance of the attractive and interesting Matt Kruger who *claimed* to be a close friend of her dead brother....

Find out more in THREATS AND PROMISES . . . available wherever Harlequin books are sold.